Inklings Book 2016

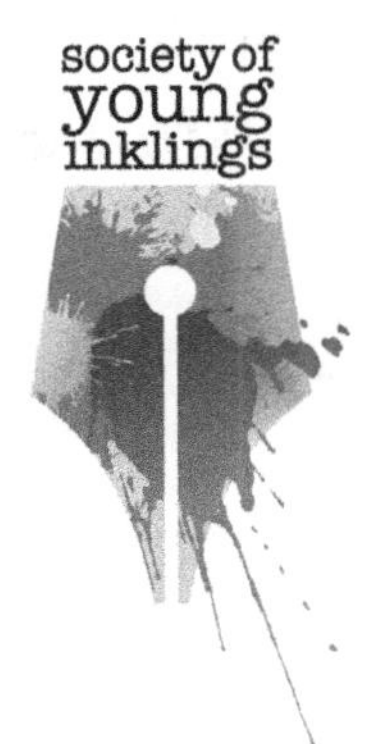

The following young authors contributed their short stories and poems to this anthology.

Juliana Baltz

Cianna Brown

Judge Cantrell

Colin Chu

Zoë Lerew Friedman

Manasi Garg

Sydney Goodwin

Erin H. Gray

Xiomara Guevara

Benjamin Hayes

Samantha James

Maya Lopez

Dillon Mareth

Jasper Micheletti

Kendra Mills

Karishma Miranda

Anabel Orozco

Natalie Sharp

Sahana Srinivasan

Rafael Stankiewicz

Samantha Vargas

Aiden Wen

Sophia Zalewski

Grateful acknowledgment is made to the following mentors for contributing their editorial guidance and letters.

Jena Brigantino

Melinda R. Cordell

Meridith Donahue

Ann Jacobus

Naomi Kinsman

Loraine McCormick

Briana Mitchell

Erica Morgan

Patricia Pinedo

Helen Pyne

Sarah Rogers

Laura Schmidt

Kavita Singh

Ashley Walker

Kristi Wright

Patrick York

Cover Illustration by: Kristin Abbott, abbottillustration.com

Copy Edited by: Loraine McCormick

Edited by: Naomi Kinsman

Printed in the USA

First Printing: August 2016

ISBN: 978-0-9910031-9-8

Contents

Poems

Special Thanks

The Inklings Book 2016 would not have been possible without generous gifts from:

San Benito Realty

Walters and Wolf

The Zanger Family

Foreword

At Society of Young Inklings, we celebrate the opportunity to showcase emerging writers. The Inklings Book 2016 is our eighth annual anthology featuring stories and poems by writers in the first through eighth grade. The collection spans a wide range of genres and is packed full of insight, humor, sparkle and fun.

Every year, our editorial team is blown away by the quality and quantity of submissions for the anthology. This year was no different. It wasn't easy, but after much deliberation, our editorial team chose twenty three pieces to publish. However, getting chosen was far from the last step for these authors—the editorial process was next!

Working closely with a Society of Young Inklings mentor, each author chose a revision focus for their piece. Then, the authors and mentors worked side-by-side to bring out the strengths in the story or poem. With each piece, you will find a letter from the mentor explaining the revision focus and approach, along with an interview from the young author. We were especially impressed this year with the reflections from the authors on the revision process. Revision isn't easy for anyone, no matter our age, because it requires us to see our work again through fresh eyes. Being willing to see where our work can continue to develop requires courage and perseverance. When we dare to do so, especially with the guidance of an editor who has the best interest of our writing in mind, we can take our work to the next level.

We know that many of the readers of this anthology are writers themselves. We hope our revision stories and strategies will send you back to your own writing with renewed passion. And, of course, it is our deepest hope that the Inklings Book 2016 provides you many hours of delightful entertainment and rich inspiration.

If you're looking for additional ways to take your own writing to the next level, check out the resources, inspiration, classes, and opportunities at www.younginklings.org.

Creating a Satisfying Ending

Ashley Walker mentored Erin Gray through a revision focused on adding surprise and inevitability to the ending of Erin's story, *Saving Billy*.

Dear Reader,

If you're opening a Young Inklings Anthology for the first time, you might be asking yourself a question: Why do book contest winners revise a prize-worthy story? My young mentee, Erin Gray, wondered this as well. Before the contest, she'd never revisited a story for this purpose, and she didn't know what to expect.

I helped Erin understand the process by acting as her editor. Together, we explored a craft element essential to the telling of her heartwarming and heroic story—namely, Creating a Satisfying Ending.

To begin, I shared with Erin one of the first and best pieces of writing advice I have ever received: *An ending should be both surprising and inevitable.*

I like to think of a story's conclusion as the bullseye on

a target. It's so satisfying to watch an archer notch her arrow, draw back her bowstring, close her eye, adjust her aim... and slip the arrow tip into that sweet spot with a resounding THWACK! Each successive step in the archer's setup ensures a successful outcome. And it increases an audience's interest.

If, on the other hand, that arrow hits the bull's eye by accident—by some baffling, loop-the-loop route—onlookers might laugh or drop their jaws in wonder, but they wouldn't feel the satisfaction of a job well done. In other words, the end wouldn't be *inevitable*.

Note that inevitable conclusions do not have to be predictable. Once the pieces are in place, it's possible for archers (and authors) to introduce an unexpected twist. On the shooting range, an opponent's arrow may be the first to find the target...But the champion can surprise everyone by splitting it down the middle. Imagine the roar of applause after that THWACK!

For authors, revision is a great time to reshape scenes to orient characters (and readers) toward the ending. Erin did this in three steps. First, she looked at her conclusion—the size and shape of the target. Next, she adjusted its distance from the starting line. And finally, she incrementally built tension across the middle of the story.

Target. In *Saving Billy*, the young protagonist, Lindy, takes things that have little worth at the beginning of the story and gives them spiritual significance and monetary value. Erin wanted Lindy to do this without help from adults (which we agreed would add tension), but it required a strong and early introduction of her story elements.

Starting Line. In Erin's revised draft, she uses her opening scene to present the problem (the failing health of beloved old Billy). And she employs her natural talent for world building to reveal Lindy's resources—the abundant art aisle in Lindy's shop and the young doodlers who will become "allies in art" in her fundraiser.

Trajectory. Across the middle of the new story, Erin adds tension and interest via a number of elements: an 'aha!' moment in which Lindy discovers a drawing to sell; a rally in which kids amass art to sell; and a final surprise in which Lindy reveals the result of her work to the adults, including grateful Billy.

Both Erin and I were excited to discover how her wonderful story, *Saving Billy*, improved after revision. We hope you will enjoy the result of Erin's hard work.

Ashley Walker

Ashley Walker is a children's book author with a confession: she didn't read much as a kid. Instead, Ashley climbed trees and flew kites and followed her interest in aviation all the way to NASA. But her biggest adventure began when she visited the local library with her kids and discovered the many exciting destinations awaiting them in the children's section. Today, Ashley writes middle grade and young adult novels, and she is a graduate student in the Vermont College of Fine Arts writing program.

Erin H. Gray

A sixth grader who loves to read and write during her free time, Erin also participates in soccer, softball, basketball, and cheerleading. Erin's favorite subjects in school are language arts, reading, and lunch, where she can talk to her best friends. Erin lives in Illinois with her mom, dad, brother, and adorable dog, Missy.

Ashley Walker: Why do you love writing?

> **Erin H. Gray:** When I am writing, I get to put myself in someone else's shoes and enjoy being them for a while.

Q: Where do you get your ideas?

> **A:** Usually I look around and see something, like a computer, and I get an idea for a story about, say, a girl trapped in a machine. So I get my ideas from the things around me… If I get blocked—and that happens a lot—I can go to the computer and scroll through writing prompts. Or sometimes, if I find a really good picture, I'll write a story about that.

Q: What changed when you revised to Create a Satisfying Ending?

> **A:** When I revised, I added in details that I forgot before—things that I missed because I was so busy typing the story.

Q: Did you think you'd change your story so much?

A: Well, I didn't really know because I haven't revised a story before. But I'm glad I changed what I dic because when I read the story a second time, it was a lot better.

Q: What advice do you have for writers who don't like revision?

A: You might not want to do it at first, but when you read back over the story, you'll see that it's worth it because it helps a lot.

Saving Billy

by

Erin H. Gray

I walked into the pharmacy and paused as the bell above the door jingled, announcing my arrival. I breathed in the deep smell of the store; actually, there were lots of different scents because right next door was the candle stand, and Aunt Etta liked to get smelly candles. Smelly in a good way, of course. The smells of blueberry Jolly Ranchers, ocean-breeze-scented candles, and raspberry scratch-and-sniff birthday cards tickled my nose.

That was my aunt, always experimenting with different ways to make the pharmacy better. My uncle was the pharmacist, and Aunt Etta was everything else. When Uncle Vinton said he wanted to open a pharmacy, Aunt Etta agreed, but only if the pharmacy could be more than just, well, a pharmacy. So it was a pharmacy/store, I guess you could say. Except, the pharmacy wasn't doing too well; the magazine shelves were lacking issues of *People and Reader's Digest*, to name a few, and the candy shelves were missing boxes of Gobstoppers and packs of Trident gum.

I swallowed and tried not to imagine the pharmacy actually

going out of business.

Aunt Etta came to greet me and led me to the back room. I dumped my backpack and coat on the floor, wincing as the colored pencils made an odd noise. I probably shouldn't have left them loose in my backpack, but the school bell had rung as I was sketching; I had to hurry to make it out before the custodian locked the doors. I was a dedicated artist, and colored pencils breaking were like my own legs breaking.

"All right!" My aunt clapped her hands together and hurried back into the store. Aunt Etta always had a job for me when I came to the pharmacy after school. My parents died a few years ago, and she liked to keep me busy to keep my mind off of them. I thought about them all the time, though: The way my mom would make disgusting scrambled eggs, but I'd eat them anyway, so I wouldn't hurt her feelings; or the way my dad would tickle me until I really, really had to go to the bathroom.

Aunt Etta, my late dad's sister, was even closer to him than I was, if that's possible. I think she tried to keep them off her mind, too. Me? To make sure I wasn't depressed all the time, I drew, worked at the pharmacy, and hung out with Billy, one of my uncle's employees. Billy was like a grandfather, best friend, and partner-in-crime to me. He was one of the few reasons I liked working all day, and that was impossible to forget.

Aunt Etta stopped in the stationery aisle and gestured to the cheaper area. Envelopes, paper, and colored pencils were all over the floor.

Sighing, I asked, "The Adamses?"

She nodded solemnly.

Cassandra Adams was our best customer, but she always brought along her nine kids, and she would send them off into the store to "have fun." "Having fun" to the Adams kids meant tearing up the store, leaving a mess for us to pick up.

I sighed and began to gather the colored pencils stuffed under the shelves.

Aunt Etta squeezed my shoulder. "I'm sorry, Lindy. What can we do? I mean, they're such great customers, and Cassandra's children are so innocent-looking…"

I gave her a weak smile. Then the doorbell jingled, and she hurried off to greet the next customer.

As soon as she had gone, I went back to work. Suddenly, I noticed something hidden under the shelves. It looked like a regular piece of paper until I looked closer. It was a beautiful picture of the front of the store. It was so vivid, so amazing, that it made me want to cry. At the bottom of the paper, written in fantastic handwriting, was the name *Marly Adams*. I didn't realize Marly, the oldest, was an artist—and a good one, at that. *Could Marly love this place as much as I do?* I wondered.

I finished cleaning the Adamses' mess, brushed the pencil lead off my hands, and went into the pharmacy area. Uncle Vint and two of his employees, Billy and Alan, were busy scribbling things down on pads of paper. I turned around, not wanting to bother them if they were working.

Then Uncle Vint called out, "Hey, Lindy, you busy? We're having a drawing contest, and we need a judge."

I chuckled. And I thought they were working! I sat on a stool across from them and said, "Okay, what do you have for me?"

Billy slid his pad across the table first. I had to admit that it was impressive—and touching. It was a portrait of me. He drew the same short, blonde-and-brown hair that I have and the outfit I had worn the

day before, a purple jumpsuit. I felt a wave of happiness as I tapped Billy's hand. He looked up.

I smiled and showed him the picture. "I didn't know you were an artist, Billy."

Billy blushed and went back to picking at the dry skin on his rough hands. I had known him since birth. When I was little, we would play "Thief," a game we made up in which one of us would steal something from the store and try not to get caught by the other. I loved the game because it was fun, and Billy loved it for that reason, too, but I could tell he enjoyed it because he got to protect the pharmacy. I liked to think it would be Billy who would run back into the store to save things if there were a fire. I didn't dare say that out loud. If Uncle Vint had heard me, he would be jealous, and sometimes my uncle could be the most sensitive person in the world.

Over the years, Billy had changed. I guess I had to accept it, but Billy wasn't as fun and bubbly as he used to be. He had heart problems in the past, but not any more. I just wished things could go back to the way they were when I was younger.

Uncle Vint tossed his notepad across the table. I tried not to laugh. He had drawn a house, and it looked like a first-grader's. So far, Billy was winning.

Alan handed me his pad. He was the youngest staff member after me, a former intern. During his term as an intern, Aunt Etta and Uncle Vinton liked him so much that they gave him a salary equal to a full-time worker's.

Alan had drawn a bunny, looking innocent as a fox crept up behind it. I gave him an approving look.

He snapped his fingers and pointed at me. It was our

handshake. I grinned and turned to the others. "So, did you guys bet on this contest? With real money?"

Uncle Vint chuckled. "Heck, no. Lindy, they knew I'd win, so they wouldn't dare."

Alan looked down at his hands and muttered, "Yeah, and the store's broke."

I froze. I could tell Billy wanted to scold Alan for bringing up the pharmacy's problems in front of me, but it was the truth. Alan was right, and no one could argue. I took a deep breath, smiled, and tried to pretend it never happened.

I announced, "The winner is…!"

All three of them made a drumroll.

I yelled, "A tie between Billy and Alan!"

I waited for my uncle's reaction, but he just cracked up, which made Alan laugh, which made Billy chuckle, which made me snort. I was a snorter. It was a habit I couldn't get rid of.

Suddenly, Aunt Etta burst into the pharmacy. "Now, what are you all doing? I was busy with a customer when I was interrupted by obnoxious chortling!"

Uncle Vint frowned. "Ettie, I'm sorry, it was my fault. Now get back to work, Alan. Billy, go wash that gray out of your hair."

Everyone chuckled, even Aunt Etta.

As the adults talked, I watched Billy get up and limp out of the back room. He reached up to fix a crooked bottle of lotion and, out of nowhere, tripped. My breath caught, but I could again breathe normally once he righted himself and rubbed his head with his palms. His eyes flew over to see if anyone was watching, and I quickly looked back at the others.

I wasn't a real employee of the store since I was too young, so Aunt Etta wouldn't let me stay as long as the other employees. So I went to the back, grabbed my stuff, and climbed into the delivery truck—the driver, Ernie, was waiting for me. I noticed a big brown stain on his button-down shirt.

I giggled. "Did you spill your coffee again, Ernie?"

He narrowed his eyes at me and drove off without answering.

The house was a short distance from the pharmacy since Uncle Vint hated driving too far. I said goodbye to Ernie and opened the front door with my key. I didn't have any homework, so I turned on the TV for background noise and made myself a ham sandwich, no mayo. Then I sat down on the couch and took out my sketchpad. I started to draw a picture of my sandwich. Soon, my snack became too tempting, and I gobbled it down before I could finish my sketch.

Thirty minutes later, I was getting restless. My aunt and uncle always came home twenty minutes after I did, since I was only in sixth grade and not allowed to be alone for too long. I picked up the phone, ready to call the pharmacy, when it rang in my hand.

I pressed the button. "Hello?"

It was Aunt Etta, and…it sounded like she was crying. She was even having trouble talking to me.

"Aunt Etta! What is it?" I demanded, trying to stay calm. *What could have happened?*

She replied, "Lindy, it's…it's Billy. Oh, he fell…he fell and hurt his back. We…we called the ambulance. Won't be home for a while. Love you." Then she hung up just as quickly as she had called.

I slammed down the phone and ran out the door, not even putting on shoes. I slid my toes into orange flip-flops that had been left out on the porch and started running. Thank you, Uncle Vinton, for not liking to drive far! I reached the store about eight minutes later. But the ambulance, with Billy in it, was already driving the opposite way.

Uncle Vint, Alan, and Ernie stood in a big huddle by the door. I ran up to them, my flip-flops slapping the pavement. Uncle Vint grabbed me and pulled me into the huddle. I started to cry. Alan was rubbing his temples, and Ernie was continuously sighing. Suddenly I was angry at my aunt for not being there. Why had she gone to the hospital without me? Didn't she know how much Billy meant to me?

After a few minutes, we broke away. Alan and Ernie went back into the store, and Uncle Vint began fixing a "Calendars—20% Off!" sign in the window. I was left alone, just standing there. I wished Aunt Etta could've been there with me, but she couldn't have left Billy alone. Running a hand through my hair, I tried not to picture the drawing contests, games of Thief, and the pharmacy in general without Billy.

The next day, Aunt Etta called the school to say I wouldn't be there. Then she drove Uncle Vint and me to the hospital.

When we walked in, I ran up to the front desk and begged to the receptionist, "Do you know where Billy Armstrong's room is? I'm a friend of his."

Uncle Vint dragged me aside. He said, "I'm sorry. William Armstrong? He's an employee of mine."

The receptionist looked surprised as she clickety-clacked away on her computer. "An employee and he's that old? I'd say he should think about retirement."

I stepped next to Uncle Vint; I was barely tall enough to see over the counter. "He doesn't need to retire," I said. "He was fine at

the pharmacy, except for some minor accidents. There weren't any life-threatening things…"

It panged my heart when I had to say "was," but I knew it was necessary. I hoped what I was saying was true—that Billy was in decent shape, and his little accidents weren't too bad for his health.

The receptionist gave us directions to Billy's room. I was the first one there. Billy was in his room, awake but silent. I gave him a big hug and then sat in one of the cozy red chairs by the bed. Aunt Etta came in a moment later, followed by my uncle.

"How are you, Bill?" asked Uncle Vint.

He got straight to the point. "I gotta undergo surgery. Don't think I can afford it, though. You might need to keep this month's paycheck; I probably won't be back to work anytime soon." He chuckled, but no one else did.

Was he really serious? If he couldn't pay for the surgery, would he die?

Aunt Etta frowned. "Excuse me? We are going to earn money for your surgery and get you back in the pharmacy as quick as a blink, Billy Armstrong," she snapped.

Very timidly, Billy asked, "How?"

Suddenly it was so silent you could hear a pin drop. If Billy didn't believe we could earn money for him, then no one else would. I looked up at my aunt, desperately (but silently) pleading for her to say something reassuring.

Luckily, she said, "I'm sure we can come up with something else. We're not helpless. Let's go green or something. How much extra money do you need, William?"

Billy croaked, "About a thousand bucks. We can't just go out and earn that, Henrietta. It's going to take a lot more. We can do something with the pharmacy, like poss bly a donation thing? That would, uh, work, right?"

I tuned them out and started to think to myself. *What if there was something I could do? I could walk dogs, make cupcakes, sell Girl Scout cookies, wash cars, whatever. If it were for Billy, I'd be glad to do it. "Thief" isn't fun with just one person.*

Just then Aunt Etta groaned, jolting me back to reality. She stormed out of the room, dragging me with her. We had to wait in the car for ten minutes before Uncle Vint finally came out.

No one talked on the ride home, but my brain was screaming ideas. I didn't decide on one 'til we got home. I collapsed on the couch, and something under me crinkled. I took it out and gasped. It was my sandwich drawing! This was perfect! My sketch reminded me of the day I found Marly Adams's drawing. The other Adams kids probably drew as well as she did! I could hire them to draw for me; then I could sell their sketches to earn money for Billy's surgery.

The next day was Thursday. Cassandra Adams loved our Thursday Sale, so I was sure she'd be there. I gathered paper and colored pencils from the house and ran downstairs to get calligraphy pens when I accidentally bumped into Aunt Etta carrying a bowl of popcorn. Kernels littered all over the carpet, and I bent down to help her pick them up. It smelled buttery, just the way I liked it. I ate a few.

Aunt Etta gave me a confused look after we stood back up. "What's with the supplies? Are you in an art class I don't know about?" she asked.

I laughed. "No, this is just..." *Quick, Lindy, you need an excuse!* I wanted to be the one who earned the money for Billy, and all on

my own. He was basically my grandfather, and if this surgery didn't happen, I'd lose a family member again. I said the first thing that came to my mind: "I was going to draw a picture of the pharmacy for Billy. That way he'll remember us. I mean, I don't know if he'll lose his memory or anything…" I didn't know how to finish it. If I didn't raise enough money for the surgery, then he might lose everything.

Aunt Etta gave me a quick hug. "That's very nice of you, Lindy. Trust me, we're doing everything we can. You know that, right?"

"Of course," I muttered, then hurried into Uncle Vint's office. Doing something about Billy was one thing. Actually talking about the seriousness of it was another thing. I could tell that even my aunt was losing faith by the second.

The next day, just as I suspected, Cassandra came into the store with nine little rug rats tagging along behind her. I counted them off as they passed me: Joey, Mitchell, Bronson, Lily, Kevin, Julia, Kylie, Tatum, and Marly. I looked at my feet when Marly passed me. I guess I should talk to her more than I do. I ignore her only because she's one of the Adamses. Only now do I realize it's a bad excuse.

"Um, Ms. Adams!" I called, and she turned around. The parade stopped behind her.

"Yes?" she asked irritably.

I cleared my throat before continuing. "If you don't want your kids with you while you shop, I realize it might be a little crowded and difficult, I can take them into the back room. I was going to draw some pictures, and I was wondering if they would like to come along."

The irritated look on Cassandra's face faded away, replaced by relief. She nodded without saying a word and thrust her kids toward me. Marly started to frown, but I quickly smiled at her—that seemed to lighten the mood a little. I looked at the other kids. The youngest few—Joey, Mitchell, Bronson, and Lily—looked so excited that I figured they'd be the ones drawing the most.

As Cassandra hurried deeper into the store, I led the Adams kids to the back room. Luckily, Aunt Etta was helping someone on the other side of the store, and Uncle Vinton was in the pharmacy. I couldn't believe how well my plan was coming together already.

I passed out paper, crayons, colored pencils, paint, and oil pastels to the younger kids, then gave the same—plus calligraphy pens—to Kevin, Julia, Kylie, Tatum, and Marly.

Before they could start, I called, "Okay, everyone, this is for a special cause, so please draw as best as you can. We need to raise money for a friend of mine who is in the hospital, and I know all of you can draw very well. Do you remember Billy? He's a very nice man, and I think we can do this to make him feel better. Okay?"

"Okay!" everyone exclaimed, except for Marly. The corners of her mouth twitched up in a smile, and she mouthed, "*I did.*" I didn't bother asking how for fear that she would get uncomfortable and refuse to help me.

Twenty minutes later, the Adams kids had drawn at least five pictures each when Cassandra came in. She hugged me and stuck twenty bucks in my pocket. That was a dollar a minute!

After the Adams family had left, I looked through the drawings. As I thought, they were all super good and could probably sell for about five dollars each. But that certainly wasn't enough for Billy's surgery, not even close.

Later, when my time at the pharmacy was up, I went through the neighborhood selling the drawings. I sold every single one and got about $225. It was fantastic—more than I had hoped for the first time around. I added my twenty-dollar bill to it and came up with

$245. Wow!

But I knew I still had to raise about $800 more. Knowing Cassandra, she wouldn't continue paying me twenty dollars every time she came to the pharmacy. So I turned to Plan B.

I was brilliant at making bracelets. That night while Aunt Etta and Uncle Vint talked about Billy and the surgery, I made as many as I could, which was luckily a lot. I sold them the next day, and, surprisingly, all the neighbors were still willing to buy from me.

I spent the entire week coming up with new ideas. I sold thing after thing, and I even got money from babysitting jobs. That wasn't shocking, though. What was shocking was that Marly knocked on my door one evening and offered to babysit with me. We spent the nights teaching the little kids how to draw, and they loved it—as did Marly. I'd never seen her so happy. I asked her how she knew Billy, but she would just blush and ignore me. I decided to stop asking, for she was content when I wasn't.

Finally, by the next Friday, I had $1,042. By then, I could tell my neighbors were getting fed up with spending money on me. On Saturday, when I didn't knock on their doors, I saw a few of them drinking coffee and relaxing on their couches.

I asked Aunt Etta to drive me to the hospital, requesting that Uncle Vint, Alan, and Ernie also come. They were confused, but I refused to tell why. I smiled. They probably had been too preoccupied with their thoughts to pay attention to what I was doing.

When we got there, I remembered Billy's room number, so I skipped down the hall and into his room.

Billy smiled when he saw me and said, "Well, how's it going, Lindy?"

"Good," I replied.

Everyone filed in after me, and I grinned. My grin got wider and wider as I reached into my pocket. The $1,000 was tucked behind my back. Then I said my speech.

"I heard about Billy's financial problems. It made me sad because we don't know what will happen to him if he doesn't get his surgery. So I went under the radar for the past week, collecting money by selling handmade stuff. I had to fight the urge to tell Aunt Etta because I know how much she loves buying handmade things from the neighbors to sell in the store. I even got Cassandra Adamses' kids to help me. The truth is, I don't know what I would do without Billy Armstrong at the pharmacy."

"So…" I held out the money, and eyes widened around me. "Here, Billy. This is for you."

Big fat tears streamed down Billy's cheeks as his shaky hand reached out to take the huge wad from me. I was wrapped in an embrace with tears from everyone dripping all over me. Aunt Etta, small, dainty tears…Uncle Vint, heavy, loud sobs…Alan, boyish but mature crying…Ernie, little squeaky-mouse sounds.

Aunt Etta leaned over and whispered, "Just imagine how proud your parents would be."

I beamed, my heart growing ten times larger.

A few days later, Billy got his surgery. Uncle Vint begged him to retire from the pharmacy. "Please, Bill, we can't risk another injury! And you can visit every day."

And Billy does visit, every day, including holidays. Even though I'm too old for "Thief," we play all the time. Whenever the Adams family comes, I am ready with pencils and paper. The neighbors make bracelets with me, and I found out that it's a lot more fun when I'm not doing it for a life-or-death situation.

Sometimes, Billy looks over at me and grins. Because without me, he wouldn't be here. And that's impossible to forget.

Building the World of the Story

Helen Pyne mentored Aidan Wen through a revision focused on world building for his original myth, *Earth and Sky*.

Dear Reader,

Earth and Sky is an original myth that draws its inspiration from Greek mythology, bible stories, fables, and folk and fairy tales. I was impressed by Aidan's confident, uncluttered writing, strong imagery, and storytelling skills. But it was the thought-provoking and complex questions he asked about what it means to be human that kept me thinking long after I'd stopped reading.

This story is about the friendship between two groups of people living in opposite worlds. They live in harmony until their choices bring about a terrible tragedy. The choices people make should always have consequences, but for readers to fully understand why Aidan's characters did what they did and how that led to the story's climactic, catastrophic conclusion, we needed more information. Thus, our revision focus was on building the world of the story.

World building is the process of coming up with all the information needed to create the world inhabited by the story's characters. This includes the history, culture, rules, physical layout and everyday realities. While Aidan had a pretty good idea about how things worked, he hadn't transferred all the information in his head onto the pages of the story. As a result, there were a few holes. So I asked him to provide more background information using exposition. In addition to coming up with the requested explanatory material, Aidan wrote several new mini scenes. These scenes accomplished a number of important things.

First, they shed light on relationships. For example, I'd been confused by the nature of the friendship between the Sky and Earth peoples. Originally, I'd assumed that it was equal and reciprocal, but as things grew increasingly tense and problematic, I realized readers needed more information to understand better how each group viewed the other. For example, why did the Sky People give so much when they got so little in return, and why didn't they fight back when attacked? Aidan tackled this like a pro, never erring on the side of over-explaining, but revealing the truth by using specific examples instead of generalities. The new material also enabled him to flesh out the lives of individual characters by diving more deeply into their voices, histories, habits, hopes, and fears. His snapshots of the Earth Child and Sky Child playing in the tall grass and of the Sky Firemaker and Earth Storyteller talking as they clean the village hearth brought these characters to life.

Second, the new scenes helped us see how things worked. In the first draft, we were told that the Sky People's magic gave the Earth People "well-being." After the revision, the vague term "well-being" was more clearly defined in a new scene that showed the Sky People working their magic by using herbs to save lives.

Third, the revision deepened the world of the story by clarifying cause and effect—like how emotion can create conflict. Initially, I didn't understand why an Earth Man would have killed a Sky Man. But when Aidan wrote a poignant scene showing how an Earth Healer lost his beloved son to an illness he believed the Sky People could have healed, I suddenly understood the pain that could cause a father to commit murder. The world of a story grows more vivid and real when abstractions become tangible and concrete.

Mythic tales are one way that humans search for meaning in life. That's why so many myths have endured for centuries. Taking time to build the world of your story can help you create an enduring and unforgettable work of fiction, too.

Helen Pyne

Helen Pyne has always loved making up stories. Growing up, she staged plays, performed magic shows, and designed haunted houses in the basement of her house. She's rappelled down cliffs in Alaska, traveled in a hot air balloon in Africa, and eaten scorpions-on-a-stick in China, but she thinks reading is the biggest adventure of all. Helen has a BA in English from Middlebury College and an MFA in Creative Writing for Children and Young Adults from Vermont College of Fine Arts. The mother of four children, she is the author of two young adult mystery novels and works as a writer and editor.

Aidan Wen

A thirteen-year-old eighth grader who attends the Nueva School, Aidan enjoys reading, programming, and playing with his younger brother. He lives with his brother and parents in Palo Alto, California, and has more than 100 family members in the Bay Area.

Helen Pyne: How did you get the idea for *Earth and Sky*?

Aidan Wen: I was reading through a list of prompts for creative writing and came across one that said: *Describe two opposite scenes.* Although I didn't feel like it was a very interesting prompt, I felt that the idea of two opposite worlds could make for an interesting story. At first, *Earth and Sky* was more of a folktale-like history of the Earth and Sky Peoples, but over time, I revised, edited, and rewrote it into what it is today.

Q: What did you like and dislike about the revision process? In other words, what was most difficult for you and what was a piece of cake?

A: Every part of the writing process from the first draft to the final draft is difficult for me. But the most difficult parts are the first and the last. I am somewhat of a perfectionist, so it's not easy for me to have confidence in my first draft and actually be able to write it. Of course, I'm never sure when the last draft is. It's hard to write a draft and call it final because it can always get better. Finding the voice of my characters/narration tends to come naturally.

Q: When did you first start writing fiction? When, where, and how often do you usually write?

A: Before I began sixth grade, I had never written fiction much before, and my writing skills were abysmal. But though I was a poor writer, I still enjoyed creative writing in my writing class. Over the course of three years, my writing skills have increased, and I now take a creative writing elective twice a week, where I can write for an hour each time. I also write in my own free time.

Q: What changed in *Earth and Sky* when you began filling in the world of your story with mini scenes and additional explanation?

A: The largest change in this round of editing was the story of the Healer. I added these scenes to expand upon the one-sided relationship between many of the Earth and Sky People. My four original characters were examples of good friendships, and I wanted to show a contrast.

Q: Was creating the world of your story a gradual process or did the ideas for your world building come to you all at once?

A: It was a gradual process.

Q: Do you have any advice for other young writers?

A: Don't be afraid to write a bad first draft and also remember that your first draft is never your last one.

Earth and Sky

by

Aidan Wen

Before history was written, two peoples shared the world. We, of the Earth, and They of the Sky.

We don't see the Sky People anymore, and we are to fault for that. But when our world was new, they would often come down from their great floating City in the clouds to visit.

For a while, peace, harmony, and happiness blessed both our peoples. The Sky People brought us light and fire, and they healed us with their magic.

Friendships formed. A Sky Firemaker warmed the feet of the old village Storyteller and his listeners. A pair of children, Sky and Earth, played tag in the fields.

***

The children were happy to play among the rabbits and tall grasses of the fields. But though the Earth held many wonders, the features of the fields soon grew dull.

One day the Earth Child asked, "You have visited my home. Can I visit yours?"

"I don't know," replied his friend, "I'm not sure we can reach it. After all, you don't have wings. And I don't think I can carry you."

The Earth Child sat down in the dry grass.

"Maybe we could make me wings. Or perhaps a Sky Person could carry me there?"

"Maybe," the Sky Child replied.

***

One morning, as the Sky People arrived in the village, the blacksmith ran forward and tugged on a Sky Man's leg. "My wife is very ill. I need you to heal her. Please."

The Sky Man looked down with concern in his eyes. "Where is she?"

The blacksmith led the Sky Man to his home. His wife lay buried under a mound of blankets on a bed. Only her pale, cold face was exposed. The village Healer sat in a chair by the bed, fumbling with small clay bottles. A cloth bag fat with herbs sat at his feet.

When the Healer saw the Sky Man, he dropped the bottles and rose to his feet. "Nothing I try works. Please, can you heal her?"

The Sky Man opened the bag of herbs and looked inside. "I can try."

The Sky Man prepared a draught with the herbs and tipped the mixture into the blacksmith's wife's mouth. Within minutes, color and warmth returned to her cheeks.

Tears appeared in the blacksmith's eyes. "Thank you! Please, name anything, and I will do all within my power to make it for you."

The Sky Man smiled. "The joy of knowing that I have saved her life is enough reward for me."

But the Healer held out the bag of herbs. "Teach me how to do that. She is the third I have seen with this kind of illness. I need to know how to treat it."

The Sky Man didn't see the greed in his eyes. "Very well. I will show you."

***

As time went on, the Earth People grew unsatisfied. They envied the Sky People with their powers of flight and healing. "What makes them so high and mighty?" they would say. "Why can't we fly, too?"

***

The Earth Storyteller and the Sky Firemaker cleaned the village hearth of ashes together, as they often did.

The sun was sinking beyond the edge of the field, its rays casting a soft orange glow over their faces.

"Tell me, do you know any good stories?" asked the Storyteller, wiping the sweat from his brow.

"I am no storyteller," replied the Firemaker, "but every young Sky Person knows the tale of our beginnings."

The Firemaker paused with his broom in the ashes.

"I believe it would be unwise to share it," the Firemaker continued. "I do not want any jealousy between the Earth and the Sky."

"There's no harm among friends," the Storyteller protested, "and I will not share it."

The Firemaker sat down on the cobbled stone rim of the hearth. He stared off into the lingering dusk. "We were once Earth People, too."

"One of us?" The Storyteller stopped his cleaning.

"Yes," the Firemaker continued. "But we changed when our ancestors discovered a treasure. We don't know its origin, but we owe it everything. Every Earth Person who looked upon the treasure, and lived by it, would rise up into the Sky as one of us. Please, keep this to yourself," he warned.

But the Storyteller, intrigued, shared the tale with the listeners who gathered at his feet each evening. They, in turn, shared it with others. And a dark spark was struck in the hearts of the Earth People. Why didn't the Sky share this treasure with them? Why couldn't they be Sky People, too?

***

The Earth Child and the Sky Child had completed their blueprint for a great tower to the Sky. The Earth Child had designed the plans, and the Sky Child had enchanted them with his magic to strengthen the structure.

"I can't wait!" the Sky Child flew a circle around the Earth Child as he walked home through the meadow. "Soon we'll stroll through the halls of the Sky Castles together, walls like flowing milk. I'll show you all the wonders of the air."

***

The Healer returned to his home after dark, his cloth bag of herbs over his shoulder, his belt full of empty clay bottles. It had been a successful day; he had treated many of the villagers, though none of their illnesses was of a serious nature.

When he opened the door, moonlight spilled onto his son, curled up on the floor. His eyes were closed. His face was pale and stiff like ice.

The cloth bag fell to the floor. The Healer lifted up his son, carried him to their bed, and gathered quilts and blankets to cover him.

His hands shook as he prepared the Sky Man's draught.

"Drink," he urged, lifting it to his son's lips. He peered anxiously into his small face, waiting for the color to return.

***

The Sky Council convened at the highest elevation of their city, a round, open-roofed room of marble and tile.

A Sky Elder rose from the great table, brow furrowed. The wind whipped his long white hair like a curtain of silk.

He looked out at the other Sky Council members. "An Earth Healer's son was taken by illness. In anger and retribution, the Healer has killed one of our citizens: a Sky Man, who helped him with his craft."

"There is no question of what we must do." A Sky Man rose across from him and spoke with a clear but wavering voice. "Recall all

our citizens, and maintain a distance from the Earth. None of us wants to cause any more lives to be lost."

"But we have friends among them," the Firemaker protested. "We cannot forsake them for the mistakes of their kin."

The long-haired Elder raised his hands, and silence descended. "We will put it to a vote."

So the vote was cast. The Sky People would draw away from the Earth, breaking all ties.

***

When the Earth and Sky Children met for the last time, the Earth Child gave the Sky Child a small bird he had carved from birch. "Remember me."

"How could I ever forget you, my friend?"

***

Without the Sky Peoples' presence, Earth fires burned low, and an illness swept unchecked through the village.

But the fire in the Earth Peoples' hearts kindled and roared.

The Earth Council held a meeting.

"My daughter is dead." One member upended a basket of porcelain bottles on the table. They rolled in every direction. A few smashed on the floor. "With the Sky Peoples' medicine, she had almost made a full recovery from her illness. But when they left, their medicines stopped working."

"They have abandoned us," said the man beside him.

"They killed my daughter," said the first council member in a voice full of rage. "Many of you have friends or family who are suffering as well—our sick and elderly.

"We could help them if we had the power of the Sky People."
Murmurs of agreement spread throughout the room.

"Yes! We must have their power."

"What were the words of the story?"

"We need their treasure. 'Look upon it and live by it,' and we will have their power, too."

***

The Earth Council issued a decree to the peoples of the Earth, seeking ways to reach the Sky.

The Earth Child stayed silent.

But every day, he returned to the fields where he and the Sky Child had played and read the plans on which they had worked so hard.

Until the day his father found him there. "What are you always looking at?" he asked.

"Nothing, Father." The Earth Child shoved the plans under his tunic, but his father snatched them away.

"What is this? Is this what you and that boy were always doing?" Grim-faced, the father rolled the plans into a tube and started toward the village.

"No!" The boy grabbed his father's arm. "Don't!"

But his father seized his collar and dragged him home. "Why are you so intent on helping our betrayers? You will stay here until this ends."

Soon, construction began. The tower grew swiftly.
Locked in his room, the Earth Child watched helplessly from his window.

***

At last, on the day the tower reached the sky, the Earth Child's father unlocked the door of his room. "Have you learned your lesson? That Sky Boy abandoned you."

The Earth Child ran past his father without a word.

***

All the soldiers of the Earth rallied into a massive army. With a great cry, they charged up the steps. The tower shook from their footfalls. The sun glinted off their swords. The Earth Child raced after them, struggling to keep up. He needed to warn the Sky Child. He needed to save him.

When he reached the great City in the sky, he found Sky Peoples' bodies strewn about the castle. Their blood stained the floors.

He ran past Sky People, their wings crumpled and bent, their eyes blank and empty. A Sky Woman still clutched a silk scarf in her fist. A Sky Elder lay slumped against a wall of milky gold, as though sleeping.

Then he found his friend. He lay in the corner of what must have been his home. His left wing was crushed and snapped in half, with the imprint of a shoe on its feathery surface. With both hands, he clutched a small wooden bird to his chest.

The Earth Child fell to the floor and gathered his friend's body into his arms. His tears stained his friend's silk tunic until the tunic was no longer the color of milk, but of storm.

"What treasure is worth this?" the Earth Child sobbed.

From the center of the once-great castle, a cry of victory rang out. The soldiers had found the treasure. A chest of gold sat on a low pillar. A soldier stepped forward, opened it, and reached inside.

"There's nothing here!" he cried.

"There must be!" Another soldier pushed forward. "We only must look upon the treasure and live by it—those are the words of the old Storyteller."

"Wait, here—" The soldier pulled a yellowed scroll from the chest. A map? A magical tome? A formula?

But when he unrolled the scroll, all it contained were five words.

Peace   Love   Charity

On Earth

Character Development

Laura Schmidt mentored Samantha James through a revision focused on character development for her lively story, *Hocus Pocus*.

Dear Reader,

I was so happy to get to help Samantha as editor for her story, *Hocus Pocus*. This story was just so much fun!

Samantha obviously spent time with this story, and it didn't need much revision. But even the best stories always have a bit of room to grow. Our revision focused on character development. Character development is the way writers weave information about their characters into the story, through both description and action. Samantha had two characters who were unique and exciting, and revision brought even more life to them!

I asked Samantha to think about three things for our revision process:

One: Can you picture these characters in your head? If yes, great! If not, take some time to try to build them up.

Once you have them in your imagination, think about physical characteristics. This includes the way they look, but it also includes things like the way their voice sounds, or the way they walk, or any odd quirks or habits. With such a great and wacky concept, there really is no limit to what these characters can be, so let's have some fun!

Two: Physical characteristics are important, and emotional characteristics are even better. The two work hand-in-hand to make characters truly light up. What are some emotional characteristics—or character traits—of Mr. Phillips and Mike? Are there parts of their personalities that you love that might need some more space in the story?

Three: Character development comes from both action and description. Where are some places you think you'd like to add character description to your piece? What about the action? Where is it helping to develop your characters and where would you like to help it out more?

Samantha and I played with some different ideas for her characters. When you're working on character development, it is often very small things that make a big impact. When she came back with her revised story, I was excited to see the changes she'd made! The best edits are ones you barely notice, and Samantha's new draft was seamless and awesome. A few small touches—little moments that tell us just a bit more about Mike and Mr. Phillips—was all it took!

I loved being the editor for Samantha's story. I hope you enjoy reading this fun and hilarious piece from this talented young author.

Laura Schmidt

Laura Schmidt is a story-obsessed word-freak who is so excited to be part of the Young Inklings team. Stories of all shapes and types have always been the centerpiece of her life, either through books, theater, or film. She personally thinks that somewhere, all stories are true, and one day she'll open a door to Narnia or fall into Wonderland. Despite this tendency, she's been granted an MFA in Writing from California Institute of the Arts and a BA in Humanities from San Jose State University. When she's not writing or inspiring young minds, Laura enjoys tackling knitting projects she will never finish.

Samantha James

Samantha is an eighth grader from Morgan Hill, California. In her free time, she enjoys playing the flute and swimming. She loves the outdoors and going on walks with her dog, Louie.

Laura Schmidt: On your own, writing for yourself or school, what is your revision process? Do you have one?

> **Samantha James:** I usually just go through it and find mistakes. I also try to find places where I could shrink down the text or expand it, and then I try to do that.

Q: Sounds good! How did you feel about working with someone else as your editor?

> **A:** I thought it was pretty fun. I like hearing other people's opinions on my story and not just seeing it through my own eyes.

Q: Do you think this process of working with an outside editor has changed anything about your process? Anything about the way you write or edit?

> **A:** A little bit. It definitely made me think about character development and how to introduce characters more.

Q: Awesome. Do you have any advice for other young writers?

A: I think, just go with your imagination. There's a lot of writing for school where you have to do it on a specific topic. With creative writing, you get to do what you want, so take advantage of that.

Hocus Pocus

by

Samantha James

Every eye in Mr. Phillips's sixth-period history class was glued to the clock, counting down to the very last second until the school day was over. At this point, there were 247 seconds until the final bell rang. After those 247 seconds had inched by at about the rate of a snail, everyone charged out the door at once, leaving a trail of binder paper and gum wrappers behind them.

When Mike was just halfway out the door, Mr. Phillips, a handicapped old man with a brilliantly white beard that went from his plump tomato-like nose down to his waistline, called out with his scratchy and worn-out voice, "Mike, can I speak to you for a few minutes?"

Mike rolled his eyes before turning around and trudging over to the teacher's desk in the back of the classroom. He had gone through far too many conversations about his grades or about his behavior with teachers, so he knew the drill.

"Take a seat," Mr. Phillips croaked.

Mike sat down, now eye-level with his teacher. Mike was made fun of for being short, so Mr. Phillips was comically short.

"I am obviously getting very old."

To Mike, this seemed to be an understatement, and it took all his willpower to keep himself from saying this out loud. The teacher continued to scan him with his brown eyes, which were half hidden beneath his wrinkly eyelids.

He finally continued, "I believe it is time that I chose an apprentice. I believe you would make a great replacement for me."

Mike sat bewildered and quickly forgot his I-will-try-harder speech he had been preparing in his head.

"Um, I appreciate the offer, Mr. Phillips," he half-mumbled, scratching his mop of blond hair, as he often did when he was confused.

"Please, call me Herman."

"I, uh, appreciate the offer, Herman, but I don't think I would like to be a history teacher."

"Well, of course, I don't want you for a history teacher! You have a C minus in my class!"

Mike shifted uncomfortably in his seat while Mr. Phillips laughed, obviously finding it amusing rather than problematic that Mike never gave a second thought to his grades, test scores, or misbehavior letters that were sent home to his parents regularly.

The teacher finally continued, as if it was the most obvious thing in the world, "I want you to replace me as a wizard!"

Mike stared unblinkingly at his teacher, momentarily peeling his eyes away to look around for a phone in case he needed to call 911 and get this man, who was clearly insane, to the hospital.

"I didn't think you would believe me, but if you want, I can prove it to you!" said Mr. Phillips.

He pulled a smooth, silvery white stick out of the sleeve of his green woolen sweater and twirled it in the air. A llama appeared out of thin air, suddenly standing near the back of the classroom, looking stupidly from side to side as if he had been there the whole time. With another twirl of the history teacher's stick, the llama was gone. Mike looked from Mr. Phillips to the spot where the llama once stood, trying to comprehend what had just happened.

"Did you ever wonder what the dinosaurs looked like?" Mr. Phillips asked, a half-grin wrinkling up his face, giving Mike the impression that he was actually enjoying this.

"I guess so," Mike replied, barely above a whisper, trying to comprehend what had happened in the past fifteen seconds and continuing to scratch his head, even though it didn't itch.

With a single wave of the wizard's silvery stick, which was apparently a wand, there was a powerful, deafening thumping sound that made the entire classroom shake. Another thump caused desks to fall over onto their sides, and a model of an Aztec pyramid fell to the ground and shattered. Mike rushed to the window and pressed his freckled nose against it, gazing at the gigantic two-story tall greenish-brown brontosaurus marching down the street! Then, as soon as the long-extinct creature had appeared, it was gone. Mr. Phillips glanced around his classroom, which easily could have been mistaken for the arena of a desk-fighting tournament.

"I can fix this," he muttered, twirling his wand.

The desks stood upright, the Aztec pyramid restored itself to its original state, and papers and pencils that had fallen out of a

cabinet floated back into place. Mike sat back down, so amazed that he felt dizzy.

"Now," Mr. Phillips continued, "you will be needing this."

He opened a drawer and handed Mike a wand exactly like his own. Smooth and unusually light, it was made of metal—a type Mike had never seen before.

"How do I use it?" Mike asked.

"It's quite simple, actually. All you do is think about what you want done, and then you say the magic words."

"Abracadabra?" Mike asked, still getting used to the feel of the wand in his hand.

"No! I don't know how that rumor got started. Hocus Pocus! You should try saying it out loud, but after a while, you can just say it in your head."

Mike waved the wand and called out, "Hocus Pocus!" He looked around him. "Nothing happened! It doesn't work!"

"Oh, right!" Mr. Phillips said, scooting forward in his chair. "It helps if you wiggle your right big toe and raise your left eyebrow! Now try again!"

Mike waved his wand, muttered the magic words, raised his left eyebrow, and wiggled his right toe. The chairs began floating upward and started spinning and flipping in the air until Mike again said, "Hocus Pocus." Then the chairs fell back to the floor.

"Excellent work!" Mr. Phillips cheered as he clapped. "I want you to practice at home, all right? Try not to tell any of your friends about this."

This seemed too good to be true until Mike realized that there was always something that ruined the fun.

"Are there any rules?"

"Rules?"

"Like what I can and can't do?"

Mr. Phillips chuckled and waved his hand through the air dismissively as if shooing away an invisible fly.

"All those silly wizards and their silly rules! I find that as long as you don't do something really crazy, no one will never know it was you! Have some fun with it!"

Mike couldn't help but smile. He simply couldn't wrap his head around the fact that he was being told there were no rules by a teacher (though Mr. Phillips was never the most rule-enforcing teacher). He stood up and thanked Mr. Phillips before running out of the classroom.

From the moment Mike had returned home, he had been sitting under a tree in his backyard, muttering, "Hocus Pocus!" He had created an elephant small enough to fit in his pocket; made his pet dog fly (which was a mistake once his dog realized how many squirrels were in the tree at the time); made it snow briefly; and changed both the color and size of a strawberry—it was now teal and bigger than a hamburger—and it tasted and smelled like sweet grape juice.

Now Mike thought about what his next act would be. He wanted to make something new, something that was big and alive! He considered making a giraffe, but he could see one at the zoo any day. Mike wanted to create something that didn't exist, like the dinosaur he had just seen out of Mr. Phillips's window.

Once he had finally set his mind on something, he waved his wand, wiggled his right toe and raised his left eyebrow, and said the words he was taught an hour or so before, "Hocus Pocus!"

Half a dozen purple trolls—each six feet tall with abnormally small ears—stood in front of him, wearing nothing but blue jeans. The trolls were bumpy, like pickles, and had thick arms that drooped down almost to their ankles, sort of like monkeys. One of Mike's new creatures advanced, grabbing Mike's wand and throwing it over the fence into the neighbor's yard.

"Hey!" Mike yelled, but not before one of the trolls in the back of the group grunted something, and all six trolls ran out of the back gate and onto the street. Mike chased them, yelling for them to come back, but with no success. Once he was through the gate and onto the street, he stopped in his tracks and watched as these purple trolls ripped up mailboxes and gnawed on tree branches. One was swinging a cat by its tail, while another was pulling doors off of cars.

Mike ran around yelling, "Stop! Stop!" but it was no use.

One of the ugly beasts started grunting and grumbling loudly, beckoning with his long, floppy arms, and all of the other trolls dropped whatever they were destroying and charged after the beckoning troll, who was now quickly walking. The mob of trolls marched four blocks—with Mike chasing after them—until they reached his school. One of the purple monsters stopped and beckoned for the other trolls to follow him. They marched straight through the doors of the school—no students were on campus this late in the afternoon—and quickly got to work wrecking lockers and chewing on textbooks! Some started kicking down classroom doors and throwing desks around.

Mr. Phillips popped out of a nearby classroom and ran to Mike, ducking to avoid being hit by a rogue chair.

"What's going on?" Mr. Phillips yelled above the loud grunting and smashing.

"I made some trolls," Mike replied, figuring that it was no use lying.

"Well, can't you make them go away?"

"No, they took my wand and threw it over a fence, and then started running around ruining stuff!"

"Well, here! Use my wand!" Mr. Phillips held his wand out in front of him, but Mike shook his head, refusing to take it.

"Why don't *you* just do it? You're way more experienced than I am!"

"No, you made this disaster, you're going to fix it!"

Mike reluctantly took the wand and waved it, shouting, "Hocus Pocus!" The trolls were still ripping the school hallway to pieces.

"It isn't working!" Mike yelled.

"Are you wiggling your toe and raising your eyebrow?"

"What? I can't hear you!" Mike screamed over the sound of the purple trolls throwing classroom doors at each other.

"YOUR TOE AND YOUR EYEBROW!"

Mike raised his eyebrow, wiggled his toe, and yelled, "Hocus Pocus!"

Finally, the trolls vanished, and whatever they were holding, fell to the ground with a *clang*. The teacher and the student gazed down the hallways that were completely ravaged and wrecked by the trolls. It looked as though there had been a magnitude 8.0 earthquake, quickly followed by dynamite explosions.

"Now if you would like to fix this mess that you made," Mr. Phillips said, loosely gesturing to the destroyed school.

Mike waved his teacher's wand and muttered the magic words. The lockers and their contents returned to their previous

positions, desks returned to the classrooms, and doors returned to the doorways. Just a minute or so later, the school looked exactly as it did before the purple pickle-like disaster-wreaking beings swept through.

"I am really sorry, Mr. Phillips," Mike stammered, his head hanging low.

"It's Herman," the history teacher corrected him.

"I'm really sorry, Herman. I didn't mean to cause any of this."

"Well, you fixed it, didn't you?"

"Yes."

"Then it's all okay. Now go find your wand."

"All right."

"And Mike?"

"Yes?"

"I would greatly appreciate it if you didn't go around hocus-pocusing any more of your crazy little friends!"

Understanding Your Main Character

Dear Reader,

I got such a kick out of Dillon Mareth's story, *Mike's Beaver Teeth*. From the beginning to end, Dillon has created a great story filled with cool things. I love how Mike wakes up with beaver teeth—and it doesn't bother him one bit. He just brushes his teeth and goes downstairs as if it's a normal day— but it's everybody else who freaks out.

All through the story, even though everybody else seems helpless and can't figure out why Mike has these humongous teeth, Mike, still totally unfazed, uses the teeth to solve several problems. Mike is cool with the teeth, and it seems like he has settled into this new way of life with no problem.

For our revision focus, we chose understanding your main character. I thought, "Isn't it crazy that Mike is the one with the beaver teeth, but, even though his family is going nuts, HE's the calm one?"

So what is going on in Mike's head, anyway?

In this story, Dillon has a good plot—that is, his main character has a problem, the problem causes other problems, and then the main character finds a solution. When the story ends, all is well again—perhaps!

But who exactly is Mike?

I do like that Mike is pretty low-key about his dilemma. But at first, he was a teeny bit too low-key. I mean, if you woke up with beaver teeth, how would that affect your day? What would you think when you looked in the mirror and saw a set of magnificent choppers filling your face? What would you say (or want to say)? What plans and schemes would you want to carry out now that you have these gigantic teeth?

Understanding your character—and getting inside their head—is very important in writing. If you are opening a book to read a 200-page story, you want to have a fun main character leading you through those 200 pages.

Imagine that you're going on a long road trip. Ideally, you want to travel with someone who's fun and makes you laugh, someone who has adventures. To be stuck in a car with a boring person is no fun.

When you think about it, a story is like a road trip. Mike could be a fun traveling companion—he just needs to share his thoughts a little more.

So as Dillon revised his story, he thought about what Mike wanted and put that in. Now the reader can watch Mike deal with this crazy and interesting problem. Dillon also dug into the scene with the dolphin on the beach and wrote more about what Mike was thinking and feeling when he freed the dolphin. As a result, the scene became deeper and more personal, and we can share in Mike's victory when the dolphin is playing in the water again.

Dillon, thank you so much for your work. I'm happy that this story is in the *Inklings Book*. Congratulations!

Melinda R. Cordell

Melinda R. Cordell is a former horticulturist, a current proofreader, and a part-time chicken wrangler (she has two red hens that don't listen). Her book, *Courageous Women of the Civil War: Soldiers, Spies, Medics, and More*, will be published by Chicago Review Press in August. She lives in northwest Missouri with two funny kids, a smart husband, a little white dog. and a very nice cat. It's a pretty cool setup.

Dillon Mareth

Dillon lives in North Bend, Washington, and just completed the third grade. Dillon enjoys playing sports and reading. He hopes you enjoy the surprise ending he crafted in *Mike's Beaver Teeth*!

Melinda Cordell: How did you come up with the idea for *Mike's Beaver Teeth*?

Dillon Mareth: I was inspired by the book *Imogene's Antlers*, which we read for an assignment at school.

Q: What do you like best about your story?

A: My favorite part of the story is when Mike frees the dolphin.

Q: When you got the revision notes, tell us what you thought about and how you used them to make the story better.

A: When I got the revisions, I already had Mike's actions, and then I thought about what he was thinking and feeling while doing those actions.

Q: What are the fun things you like to do during an average week— for instance, sports, reading, writing, making Vine videos?

A: On an average week, I like to play sports, like baseball, soccer, and football. I love to read. My favorite book series is *The Imaginary Veterinary*.

Q: What kinds of stories do you like to write?

A: I like to write fantasy stories because then you can come up with new stories and new imaginary stuff that could not normally happen.

Q: How did you hear about the Inklings contest? How did you get ready for it?

A: My teacher, Mrs. Ang, told me about the Inklings contest and asked me if I wanted to submit one of my stories. I got ready for it by picking a story from an assignment and then making it into a bigger story.

Mike's Beaver Teeth

by

Dillon Mareth

One Saturday, Mike woke up feeling funny. He looked in a mirror and saw he had beaver teeth. He was so shocked that he shook for a few seconds, but then quickly recovered. He thought this was the worst thing that ever happened to him. He wanted to forget about it, so he figured he should get ready for the day.

Brushing his teeth took a lot longer. When he was done, he couldn't close his mouth. When he went downstairs, his family was shocked. His dad fainted.

"Why do you have beaver teeth?" screamed Mom.

He tried to reply, but it was too hard. His teeth kept getting in the way.

Mike tried to think of a way to make his beaver teeth go away. He had an idea to go to the dentist, and he told his family his idea. They thought it was a great idea.

Mike's mom and dad took him to the dentist, but the dentist couldn't figure out why Mike had beaver teeth. After the dentist, Mike's dad had an idea and tried to use sandpaper to grind down his

teeth, but it didn't work. Mike's older brother looked on the Internet to see if anyone else had this problem. No one did.

Mike went outside, and his dad asked him to cut firewood with his teeth. Mike was really fast at cutting wood. He could cut a log in half in just one minute.

Down at the beach, Mike saw a dolphin stuck in a net. It was squiggling and crying for help. Mike loved dolphins. They were his favorite animal, so he knew he had to save the dolphin. He used his teeth to cut the net and free the dolphin. When the dolphin was free, it swam away and jumped out of the water. Mike thought it was saying, "Thank you for saving me."

Later, Mike went back inside for dinner. He found it was easier to eat his thick, juicy steak because he could chew better. He thought maybe it wasn't so bad to have beaver teeth after all.

After dinner, Mike watched TV with his family and then went to bed.

On Sunday morning, Mike found he'd lost his beaver teeth, and he had his regular teeth. When he went downstairs, his family was super happy that he was back to normal. But when he came into the room, they saw that he had a beaver tail!

Connecting the Dots

Kristi Wright mentored Sydney Goodwin through a revision focused on adding key details in Sydney's hope-filled story, *Unspoken: A Story of the Underground Railroad*.

Dear Reader,

Sydney Goodwin's *Unspoken: A Story of the Underground Railroad* is such a beautiful and hopeful tale. It's about a young girl who takes huge risks to bring food to a runaway slave hiding in her barn. Though they never meet, they build a connection that neither will ever forget. I was immediately caught by this story and delighted to work with Sydney on her final revision. Already, her voice was captivating, and the emotional impact of the story was very strong. We decided to focus on connecting the dots for the reader as a revision focus.

Sometimes as writers we forget to give our readers important information necessary to keep them engaged in our stories. The last thing we want is for a reader to pop out of our story by asking, "Why?" Like a connect-the-dot drawing, we want to masterfully take our readers along as the story unfolds until they see the full picture!

Connecting the dots for the reader can be challenging because as writers, we are so close to our stories that we already have connected the dots in our heads over and over again. That's why some dots never make it to the paper.

One simple strategy for connecting the dots is to ask multiple people to read your story and then give you a list of questions that stopped them in their reading or even just made them pause. Then you can brainstorm ways to add internal or external dialogue, or even action, to "answer" your reader's questions.

You can also try to find these missing dots yourself. Often, connect-the-dot moments require following the logic as characters make decisions or draw conclusions. So print out your story and then read it (out loud, if possible). Highlight every time your character makes a decision or draws a conclusion. Then look at the text leading up to that moment and double check whether you gave your readers enough evidence or logic for them to follow why the character made that particular choice. Add in the appropriate "dots" if necessary.

During revision, Sydney added a number of these "dots" to her story. For example, she added logic to explain why Tara, her main character, decided to eavesdrop on her parents. Tara overheard some important information, which helped her determine that the person hiding in the barn was, in fact, a slave. Sydney also added some crucial details so that readers understood the significance of the big dipper as a navigation tool for runaway slaves. These details and more enhanced an already beautiful story.

It's been such a pleasure working with Sydney Goodwin. I'm so excited for you to read her heartfelt and impactful tale. I hope that you will have fun connecting the dots for your readers in your own writing!

Kristi Wright

Kristi Wright is the author of the middle-grade, futuristic *Basker Twins in the 31st Century* series. She writes both middle-grade novels and picture books. In addition to her futuristic novels, she loves to write stories that are magical or whimsical. She conducts writers' workshops at elementary and middle schools that focus on sensory detail and a strong character point of view. She is an Assistant Regional Advisor for the Society of Children's Book Writers and Illustrators. A Young Inklings mentor, she lives and writes in Santa Clara, California.

Sydney Goodwin

Sydney is ten years old and heading into fifth grade. In addition to writing, she loves soccer, dance, and reading. Her favorite soccer position is outside defender, her favorite dance is contemporary hip-hop, and her favorite book genre is historical fiction. She's a fan of the *American Girl* books. If she could visit anywhere in the world, it would be Paris, France. Sydney lives in Livermore, California, with her mom, dad, and fourteen-year-old sister.

Kristi Wright: How did you come up with the idea for *Unspoken*, and what's your favorite part?

Sydney Goodwin: Writing about the underground railroad was a classroom project. My favorite part of *Unspoken* is the ending. I love how it's so calm and peaceful!

Q: How long have you been writing?

A: I've been writing since first grade. Mostly I write modern/contemporary stories.

Q: What's your favorite part of writing?

A: I like making up characters and creating adventures and drama!

Q: How was it revising *Unspoken*? Did the idea of connecting the dots for the reader make sense? Can you use this in future writing?

> **A:** It was kind of hard because I don't like to do stuff a second time. So, I was a little frustrated. But "connecting the dots for the reader" made sense. And I think the end result is good. Much better than before. I still don't like to edit, but I think I might be a little less frustrated in the future by the revision process because I'll remember that the outcome is good.

Q: What did you like and dislike about revising? What did you learn from this process that you can use in your next revision?

> **A:** I liked the end product, and I disliked actually having to revise! But I think I'll try to be more willing to revise in the future. And I'll try to look at my stories to see where I might connect the dots for the reader.

Q: What advice do you have for other Inklings who may not want to revise?

> **A:** If you revise, the story will be better than it was before! And always try your best!

Unspoken: A Story of the Underground Railroad

by

Sydney Goodwin

It was a warm fall afternoon, and I was in the fields milking my cow Gilda.

"Come on," I yelled at her.

I then glanced up from the pail. Five strange men were walking across the lawn. They had angry faces, which frightened me; butterflies danced in my stomach. I wanted to yell, "Hey," but I kept silent. I didn't want to cause a scene, plus I didn't know who they were. They carried a strange flag that I think is called a *con-fed-er-ate* flag, but I had no idea what it meant. I quickly walked away, but my mind was still on the men.

Well, they're not bothering me, so I might as well continue my chores.

"Now, now chica," I said to the smallest chick who was trying to climb up my leg as I was feeding her.

I turned my head and smiled at my mom. Suddenly, I realized

that a blanket with a pretty pattern hung from the fence. *Hmm, strange, was that always there?*

"Tara, honey, go get some veggies for my stew," I heard Ma call from the porch.

"Yes ma'am," I called back as I turned toward the barn. "Bye my little chickies," I said to the whimpering chicks. "Hmmm hmm hmm," I hummed as I gathered tomatoes, onions, carrots and many other veggies for my mom's stew. Then a noise interrupted my humming. I shut my mouth and listened. I heard the sound of brushhhhh brushhhh coming from the corn husks. My face turned from tan to bright red.

"Hello?" My voice cracked so much it sounded like a campfire. No one answered. But I did hear a faint swallow. "Okay, that is it!"

I ran from the barn, dropping the veggies as my hands flailed in the air. With my mouth wide open and eyes as big as a bowl, my breath cut short, and I tripped over the stairs and stumbled onto the porch. I crawled over to the front door and stood up. I laid my ear against the door of my house to see if I could gather a little insight on the person. (If it was a person, anyway.) I listened deeply to the conversation my parents were having inside the house.

"I laid the quilt out this morning," I heard my mother whisper secretively. "So we may notice a little..." Her voiced suddenly dropped, "strange activity coming from the barn."

My mouth dropped open.

Aha! The quilt was important. So it is definitely a person in the barn, but what was so bad or scary about them that my parents were whispering?

Thoughts circled in my head about the person in the barn.

I decided to open the door and go inside my house since I looked weird standing outside with my ear pressed against the door.

Oh no, the veggies for the stew!

When it was time to pray for dinner, I could not pay attention. My thoughts were still on the catastrophe in the barn!

What if it were a slave in the barn? What if it were someone who wanted to hurt me or what if it were a thief or an outlaw or even a monster? No, not a monster. How would the monster have anything to do with a quilt? Besides monsters did not exist…hopefully!

I weighed the options.

If it were someone trying to hurt me, wouldn't they have already at least tried to hurt me? And if it were a thief, why would he be in the corn husks?

It just didn't make any sense. I had two possibilities off the list, but I still had two more to go.

Okay, so what about outlaws? Surely if they knew I were there, they would have scattered. Plus, I'd heard about this new rumor that slaves used the big dipper to find their way. I remembered seeing the dipper last night, so it must be out tonight, too.

It all made sense now. It had to be a runaway slave. By the time the prayers were over, I decided that I would go out and give him or her a piece of my bread from dinner. I hid a slice in my napkin, and after dinner, I got a lantern and headed to the barn.

The chilly air sent shivers down my spine, but I continued toward the barn. The sky was clear, and I could sharply see the big dipper. I started to feel queasy from the wind and the fact that I was actually doing this! Still, I headed full speed ahead to the barn, hoping that it was a slave who was in hiding.

I stepped up onto the wooden floor in the barn. I tiptoed to the corn husks and laid out a napkin with the bread. I waited to see if someone would come out, but no one came, so I left the napkin and bread there. I decided to return the next day before chores to pick up the napkin and bread if it was still there. I snuck back into the house, and I felt like a hero. Nobody even noticed that I had been gone. I sighed quietly with relief.

The next day, the bread was gone, so every night I went to the barn to feed the slave. From pie to chicken, cornbread, and biscuits, I fed a bit of everything to the slave, and every day the food vanished.

One warm day about two weeks later, I had just finished milking our cows, when I again noticed strange men on horses stomping on our lawn. But these were not the same men from before—there were two men this time, and they had a third horse along with them. They looked mad at something, but I didn't know what.

I hid behind the barn, staring at the men.

Did they want to hurt us?

They got off their horses and stomped inside our house. I tiptoed behind the men. They pulled out a poster of a runaway slave. They were here to get the slave. I knew that the look on my face would give away the secret, so I slid into the nearest closet. I peeked through a crack in the closet. The men shouted, bargained, and screamed. My Pa, Ma, Nana, and Pop looked like they had no clue what the men were yapping about, but I could tell by the look on my mother's face that she was bubbling with fear inside. The slave catchers begged and begged, but my family would not crack. I knew they had something to do with the slave. The men even offered a $200 reward! But my parents just shook their heads.

The men marched out of the front door and back onto the wooden steps. I heard a loud crash and knew it was a wooden plank breaking from the weight of the men.

I heard faint muffled voices from outside and then a loud, "We ain't gonna get no cash."

I slipped out of the closet and giggled. Then I ran back outside to see the stubborn men leaving. I quickly glanced back toward the barn as my smile vanished.

What if the slave did not get a chance to escape?

My parents had risked their lives to make sure the slave was safe and so would I. I snuck out to the barn later that night. I hadn't retrieved the napkin today because of all the chaos. I was scared for the slave; I didn't know if they had escaped. Once inside the barn, I noticed a cute little figurine—a corn-husk baby—and I realized that it was wearing a dress made from the napkin! The slave had left it behind. For me! The freezing cold suddenly turned into a warm and cozy place. I smiled and the baby seemed to smile back at me.

That night, I lay in my bed with the baby in my hand and the quilt on my bed. I looked out of my window at the big dipper and knew it would guide the slave to safety. I slipped off to sleep and dreamed about the unlikely friendship that was, Unspoken.

Character-Specific Dialogue

Jena Brigantino mentored Zoë Friedman through a revision focused on dialogue in Zoë's clever story, *My One-Inch-Tall Life*.

Dear Reader,

Zoë Friedman's story *My One-Inch-Tall Life* is a unique story about a tiny character with a big problem. Zoë's clever word choice allows readers to slow down and enjoy the beautifully written story.

Zoë worked on character-specific dialogue in her revision process. A combination of dialogue and action brings a scene to life. Authors also use dialogue to show readers a character's personality. When writing dialogue, don't forget to describe what the characters are doing in a scene. One character might talk slowly while sighing or mumbling to oneself, and another character might shout loudly in short sentences.

Zoë did an excellent job of using both action and dialogue to bring scenes to life and to show characters' personalities. I know you'll enjoy *My One-Inch-Tall Life*. Happy reading!

Jena Brigantino

Jena Brigantino grew up playing outdoors in California where she dreamed up stories featuring animals. She wishes she could have participated in an Inklings program as a child. As Managing Director of SYI, she strives to extend the opportunity to as many children as possible. Jena holds a BA in Creative Arts with a minor in Education from San Jose State University. In her spare time, Jena enjoys spending time with her big Italian family where memorable stories are constantly shared...loudly!

Zoë Friedman

Zoë is in third grade at Huff Elementary. She plays soccer, skis, and loves singing, acting, and reading. Zoë adores the *Harry Potter* series, and it inspires her writing. She wants to thank her second-grade teacher, Ms. Luongo, for encouraging her imagination and creativity and supporting her creative writing.

Jena Brigantino: When did you start writing?

> **Zoë Friedman:** Four years ago with my neighbor. We would write stories with illustrations. The first story we wrote was about mice with powers.

Q: Where do you like to write?

> **A:** I like to write outside on a bench on my porch. I like writing outside because when I'm outside, I get inspired by nature.

Q: How do you come up with your ideas?

> **A:** Sometimes I get ideas from other books and then I put the ideas in my own words. Sometimes ideas just pop into my head, and I have no idea how they get there.

Q: How do you feel about the revisions you made in *My One-Inch-Tall Life?*

> **A:** I like how my story turned out.

Q: What advice do you have for other Inklings who don't like revision very much?

> **A:** I felt the same way at first, but I wanted my story to be the best it could be. I recommend playing games to get through revisions. Inklings games help you think about stories and how to put things together. Plus, they're fun!

Q: What are you writing now?

> **A:** I'm writing a "Cinderella Continues" story. It's about the real life of Cinderella and the Prince after they get married. I don't think they will live happily ever after.

My One-Inch-Tall Life

by

Zoë Lerew Friedman

Chapter One—My Birth

It all happened on May 22, 2008. I was born in the hospital. Once my mom gave birth to me, she didn't even see me. The doctors took me out of the room right away. A day later, I came out of the NICU, and my mom and dad saw me for the first time.

"She's so small," my dad whispered into my mother's ear.

My mom hugged me, but it was hard. I was one inch tall!

My mom and dad took me home after a week at the hospital. They sat me in a peanut shell with a small piece of spaghetti for the seatbelt, and the peanut shell was the car seat.

On the way home, my mom kept asking herself why I was only one inch tall. Then something clicked in her mind. She remembered that before she had me, she drank a potion when she was ill that the town's elder healer gave her.

When we got home, my mom took me to my room, but there was a big crib, so I slept in the peanut shell and had a leaf as a blanket.

***

Two years passed, and I was still only one inch tall. Once I was two years old, my parents told me I could have a butterfly to take me places. I jumped up and down on the palm of my mom's hand. I was so excited!

Chapter Two—Life

One day, I was flying on my butterfly, Sugarcup, and she crashed. We were fine, but we had no clue where we were. Back at home, my parents were crying. I had been in the forest for a day, and they didn't know where I was.

Back in the forest, I wept and wept and wept. Days passed, and I was no closer to finding my way home. The forest was very different from home. In the morning, I would jump on lily pads and stand on them and just let the water take me places. In the evening, I would eat berries that I would find in the wild.

I lived in the forest for two years. By now I was four, and I would wander off in the forest by myself.

Chapter Three—The Boy

I had amazing, fun times in the forest, but I missed home and tried to keep my mind off that. Eight years passed, and now I was two inches tall. To me, it was a big difference. By now, I was twelve. I couldn't believe it!

One day, I was flying on Sugarcup, and she landed in a new part of the forest. She looked frightened. She threw me off of her back and flew on top of a tree.

"Sugarcup," I cried.

Suddenly, a boy my age came running up to me. He lifted me off the ground, and I looked into his eyes; they sparkled.

He looked back into my eyes and said, "Good morning, ma'am."

I said, "Good morning."

The boy mumbled to himself, "I've never seen anyone this small."

Sugarcup flew down from the tree and perched on his hand. He flicked her away.

I had to shout to him because I was so small, "Don't do that! That's my butterfly!"

The boy put his hand down and Sugarcup flew back onto his hand.

I shouted, "My name is Zoë!"

The boy said, "My name is Jonathan." Then he paused and asked me, "Why are you so small?"

I answered quietly, "My mom drank a potion from our town's healer when she was ill, before she had me, and it made me so small."

Chapter Four—The Potion from Jonathan

"I know how to make you normal size," Jonathan exclaimed.

"How?" I asked.

"Just drink the same potion your mom drank," he said.

"Do you have the potion?" I asked.

"Yes," replied Jonathan.

"But how?" I wondered.

"You won't believe this. My grandmother is the town's healer. She is the one who gave your mom the potion."

He gave me a glass, and I drank the green liquid slowly. Suddenly, I felt something weird. The green liquid ran down my throat. It tasted bad, but I swallowed it down. I felt my body growing. My mind was spinning. I looked down and I was normal size.

Jonathan told me he could take me home. I couldn't believe I would see my parents. A day later, he took me to my house, and I saw my parents for the first time in ten years.

My parents were reading when I walked in the door. They looked up with stunned eyes. I cried happy tears when I saw them.

"Zoë?" my mom whispered.

"Yes," I sobbed, "I'm finally home!"

They hugged me, and I told them all of my amazing adventures but also about my sadness in missing them. I hugged them so tightly; I did not want to let go. I had so much fun being one inch tall, but it was nice to be normal size and back with my parents.

Pacing

Meridith Donahue mentored Manasi Garg through a revision focused on pacing in Manasi's action-packed story, *The Girl with the Light-Up Shoes.*

Dear Reader,

    The Girl with the Light-Up Shoes is an action-packed story. Manasi dreams up a world where science begins to replace magic, setting the stage for a dramatic climax and emotional, yet satisfying, resolution.

    Because of the story's intensity, Manasi and I focused on pacing. I wanted to add suspense in the scenes leading up to the climax and make sure each scene in the story was balanced with the arc as a whole. A story should have a good mix of scenes that are fast-paced and ones that are slower-paced, but every scene should work together to build to an exciting climax.

    Manasi and I worked together to slow a few scenes down and add tension where it was needed. Manasi achieved this by adding sensory details and dialogue.

    Sensory details are easy to add to your story. Think about

a scene you'd like to work on. Close your eyes and explore your story's setting. What do you see? Smell? Taste? Touch? Hear? When you're finished with the exercise, make a list of all the new things you noticed. Then, see where you can add more sensory details to your story. Adding detail can slow down a scene that needs to be fleshed out and can also make the story more real for your reader.

You can use dialogue to adjust the pace of your story, too. Manasi amped up the tension in her story by breathing life into an old conflict between two characters. One character's dialogue is short and clipped, while the other's sentences are longer and pleading. The differences in speaking style serve to add tension and give the scene a balanced pace.

Think about another scene in your story. What are the characters saying to each other, and how do they say it? Depending on the type of story you're writing, shorter and longer sentences can add suspense and slow down the pacing or speed it up. Experiment with different sentence lengths to see how the pacing changes. In addition, carefully crafted dialogue can add character depth, tension, and intensify the conflict.

Adding sensory details or dialogue can help balance your story's pace. It's important that each scene flows well so the story works as a whole. Taking a look at your story's pacing is a big step, and once you do, you'll be on your way to a well-paced story.

Meridith Donahue

Meridith Donahue's ove of books and writing began at an early age, when she would take as many books out of the library as she could carry. In junior high, she began taking voice lessons and auditioned for her very first musical. Ever since then, she's been on stage performing in or choreographing plays and musicals. She co-led her college's comedy improv team and got a poem published in her school's literary magazine. She's never given up on either passion and got a BA in English Studies from Northern Illinois, as well as an MFA in Writing for Children and Young Adults from Hamline University. When she's not teaching, writing, or performing, you can find her reading or watching BBC shows.

Manasi Garg

Manasi is an average antisocial teen who carries a book with her everywhere and prefers interactions with the characters in her imagination to conversations with real people. Her "to-be-read" list is longer than the miles she has to (ironically) run at swim practice. She dreams of being surrounded by nothing but nature and her own thoughts and a pen and paper. She doesn't have a single clue where her future will lead her, but she hopes that writing and reading will always be a huge part of her life. (Also, she is still waiting for her Hogwarts letter. What, is it lost in the mail or something? If anyone knows anything about it, please contact her immediately.)

Meridith Donahue: How did you like the revision process?

> **Manasi Garg:** It was hard, but it was definitely fun, too, to get inside my characters' heads and put myself at the setting and the location.

Q: What was your favorite thing that you were able to add as you revised?

> **A:** The dialogue between Rose and Cyra added emotion because this story is not the most emotional, but that added good depth to their characters and gave a foreshadowing of what might happen next.

Q: What advice do you have for other writers who don't like revision?

A: I don't know if I'm qualified to give advice, but I'd say it's hard. In the end, it's worth it. It can be fun. If you don't like that section, there's a reason you're revising it because you're making your story the best you can possibly make it.

Q: What Hogwarts House would you be in?

A: I'd probably be in Ravenclaw because that's what the Pottermore quiz said. I wouldn't mind being in any of the other houses, actually.

Q: What do you think your favorite Hogwarts class would be?

A: Probably Charms or Transfiguration, especially Charms—that's cool. But if I could become an Animagus, that'd be cool, too. I'd probably be a bird or a wolf.

Q: Why do you enjoy writing?

A: It's a way for me to bring the characters in my imagination to life. The same reason I love reading—an escape from real life. It's a creative outlet for me.

Q: When did you start writing?

A: I don't know. I never officially considered myself a writer, but it's been a hobby since I was maybe in second grade.

Q: What do you do if you feel stuck?

A: Usually, either I try to get inspiration from my favorite books or see what my favorite author does when they're stuck. Otherwise, I take a break from writing.

The Girl with the Light-Up Shoes

by

Manasi Garg

The city is dark. The only light comes from the streets, where a little girl dances around on the streets staring at her new light-up shoes, at the red, white, and blue glowing up like blaring sirens of the police that ruthlessly chase people down. Her mother looks on, nerves jangling. It's late—nearly past midnight and well past the curfew. They are openly breaking the curfew.

The Cardens are already a targeted family. The mother and daughter should not be out this late, and the little girl with her strange amethyst eyes and her bright light-up shoes is not supposed to be alive. Letting her dance on the streets is foolish. It could cost them their lives—or worse.

But to give this little five-year-old girl a taste of childhood, a taste of freedom and the feeling of love, even if only for a few years, is enough to risk everything.

The mother is a Carden, after all. She may be disowned from the great family, but losing your family's love and respect does not

mean you don't share the same blood. And right now, her blood is the most valuable thing she has left. Except for her daughter. Because after everything that's happened, this little girl is all Rose has left to live for.

"Come on, baby. We need to go home," says Rose gently.

"Okay." The toddler clutches her mother's hand tightly, gazing down every few feet at her flickering shoes.

They walk quickly down the black streets, unseen eyes following them with a cool, hard gaze. The two take shortcuts through alleys and other grimy corners of the city where authorities never are, where people dressed in rags curl up in the shadows, staring blankly at the sky as if they've lost everything. *They probably have*, Rose thinks, and she shudders.

Thirty minutes later, mother and daughter stand in front of a small, dirty house, the little girl still in awe of her new shoes, watery shafts of light painting strange whirls of color on the ground. The mother stares at the dirt-stained walls, lost in thoughts of the past. To an outsider, nothing would look too unusual. But up close, Rose is clenching and unclenching her hands, her eyes sweeping the shadowy woods surrounding the cottage.

It's silent. Too silent.

But nothing moves.

And that's when Rose makes her first mistake. She disturbs the stillness, the darkness, that was her protection. She grabs her daughter's hand, and the two walk softly down the path. The only noise is the soft jangle of keys as Rose fumbles for them.

Then a rustle in the bushes. A faint footstep. A human heartbeat.

A white flash, an explosion of sound, and a minute later, four bodies are lying on the ground. There are no neighbors around to hear or see, no light to shed on the barely breathing.

The little girl is still standing, looking in horror at her mother and the others—three men—clothed in the stark gray of people she was taught to avoid, tendrils of pure energy curling around her body and her eyes glowing silver. She shudders and screams and feels streaks of terrible, beautiful power spark up and down her arms, and her body feels like it's blazing up.

Then rough hands pick her up and carry her over the rocky terrain and onto a path next to the woods. She struggles against the person, fiercely, and screams, but her captor clamps a hand over her mouth and holds her firmly. The little girl stares up at the black sky and the black trees and all the darkness. There is no one here to see her, no one to save her.

The forest taunts her. She stares at the trees, and they become shadowy giants leering down at her, seeming to hold dark, ancient secrets, and, suddenly, the little girl is filled with a strange desire to solve the forest's mysteries. She starts trembling and shaking even more—not out of fear but out of a burning pul toward the trees.

Then she lashes out and kicks her captor in the stomach as hard as her five-year-old legs can. Sparks jolt up the captor's stomach, and she lurches forward, snarling after the little girl, but the little girl scrambles to her feet and runs to the forest's edge on unsteady legs. The ground is uneven, and she can feel the rocks cutting through her thin shoes, but she doesn't care.

If I get to the forest, I'll be safe, the thought cuts through her jumbled mind.

It doesn't make sense; she can't explain it—every story she's ever heard has warned of forests and their dangers. But she also knows that silently complying with her captor is even more dangerous. So she runs. Runs like she never has before.

It's cold, and the air cuts through her like shards of ice, but her legs are burning, and she is on fire, igniting with fear and hope. And even though she's sprinting toward the gloom as hard as she can, she feels fingers brushing her back and hands curling around her, drawing her in, pulling her. Her head is hurting, but she can smell the pine and musky forest scent. So the little girl puts out an extra spurt of energy, and when the only thing that stands between her and the trees is a few feet of craggy rock, she leaps!

And suddenly, the same powerful energy sparks up again, fierce bolts of energy zinging at her captor who shouts with rage and stumbles back. It propels the little girl into the silent trees and relative safety, and she gasps with relief.

Yes! I made it! she thinks.

She leans against a tree trunk, her breath going in and out in short puffs that look ghostly white in the midnight-painted clearing. It's the only sound she hears in this strange forest. But she doesn't notice.

I'm alive, she thinks, *and I'm free*. Her head lolls to the side, and her breathing steadies.

But the whole forest is holding its breath, watching, waiting, for the next, inevitable, turn of events.

Because while the girl is slumped against a tree trunk, drained of energy and half-asleep, her captor is not. The magic slowed her down, but it didn't stop her. Besides, what she is about to do doesn't really require any energy.

The captor tosses something into the woods—a spidery device that glows strangely against the black canvas of the trees. It scurries into the woods, hunting.

And it finds its target.

Ten minutes later, the little girl feels rough hands holding her once again, feels the rocky terrain and feels the same, primitive, allure to the forest. She sees the midnight sky and tastes the cool night air. But now there is nothing she can do to escape. Her hands and feet are bound with an odd, flexible metal rope that tightens whenever she moves.

A prisoner. It's almost laughable. A five-year-old, notorious enough for her own guard and handcuffs.

And so, she is led to a strange glossy-black contraption that vaguely resembles a car.

"She's here," says the rough hands' owner.

"Bring her in," murmurs a melodious voice.

The five-year-old is shoved inside, and she trips over the strange ropes, feeling herself falling until cool black hands catch her.

"Be more careful, Yukimura. Remember how you got here. This child is just the beginning, and she is the most important," the voice says in a different language.

But although the girl does not understand what she is saying, she hears the voice's poisonous sweetness.

"Yes, Your Highness."

Yukimura unbounds the child's handcuffs, and then carefully seats her across from the woman with the poisonous voice.

The little girl looks up—and gasps. This woman is beautiful—

even more than her mother—with her deep, warm-brown skin and delicate, high cheekbones. Her hair shimmers white, but her face is young, and her smile is warm.

Perhaps life won't be so bad, the girl thinks. Perhaps the forest…it must have been a mistake. There is no way that life would've been better had she successfully escaped. She feels grateful that this woman has given her a chance.

Yet when the woman turns her eyes on the little girl, the child feels a cold shock. Her eyes are pale blue and cut through her like shards of ice on a winter's day, and the little girl remembers the bodies on the ground and the looming trees and silver energy and her mother's fair hair fanned out on the ground as she lies still.

"Mama! What did you do to her? How could you just leave her there? MAMA!" the girl wails.

The queen feels a red-hot anger well up in her, burning her icy insides, so unlike her usually cool stance. She has done so much to rescue this foolish child from a horrible life and a horrible mother, done so much to save her from her own blood, and this is how she responds? And that stunt with Darelyn Forest and the magic? The fact that she even got that far is unbelievable. Does this child even know what would have happened to her if she weren't so essential?

But the queen takes a deep breath and says, as kindly as she can, "Adira, darling, your mother is dead. I will be your mother now. Try to understand that this is for the best. You don't know who your mother was, or what she did. You don't understand where she was from. You deserve better, Adi, much better."

"No! I want MAMA! Not you!" she shrieks.

The woman sighs, "Darling, I tried to be patient with you. I really did. But I refuse to deal with the bratty whining of a simple child. Yukimura, take her away. Move her to the bedroom near Princess Emilia's."

Rough hands pick up Adira once again and lead her away.

"NO! NO! STOP! Mama, wake up, please, PLEASE, Mama, wake UP! WAKE UP MAMA! PLEASE!" she screams until her throat goes dry. And then she sobs more, wishing again and again for the energy that almost saved her, and wishing for her mother, who surely would save her.

But Adira is forced to walk away into the darkness.

***

There is a slight stir on the ground in front of the cottage as Rose tries to get up and save whoever is calling her. But she can't move. Something is trapping her—a strange force field of sorts—and draining her powers. Magic is powerful, but science is more so. There is nothing more she can do.

"Hello, Rose. It's been awhile," says a familiar voice.

The only response are groans of pain.

"Oh, excuse my rudeness. It's me, Cyra. Remember?"

Yes, thinks Rose, *I do remember.*

"I was your best friend—or, at least, I was until you left me for your family. The same family you hated. And, of course, there is the matter of you and Stefen," the queen says emotionlessly, although she still feels the sharp pain of betrayal even five years later.

Rose grunts.

"Good, good. Well, I just wanted to tell you that you are going

to die now. Good night."

Something finally registers in Rose's mind.

"Adi-Adi-ADIRA! WHAT DID YOU DO, Y–," Rose gasps finally, struggling against whatever strange force binds her.

"Don't worry. Your daughter will be fine. In fact, I expect she'll be quite happy in her new home," smirks the queen.

"NO! ADI! MOMMY'S COMING! ADIRA!" she screams with everything she can.

"Goodbye, Rose," Cyra says simply.

"NO! Cyra, please, PLEASE! The Cyra I knew would never have done this. She never…she wouldn't…she was kind and intelligent and–," screams Rose.

"The Cyra you knew is dead," the queen laughs sadistically, enjoying Rose's pain. "And soon you will be dead too. Perhaps the two of you fools can reminisce together."

"I hope you rot, Cyra," Rose snarls. "I hope crows pick your bones clean and your remains reduce to ashes until you are nothing more than…," she chokes.

""Goodbye, Rose."

Then, with a sharp flick of her wrist, the queen summons two people forward. A swish of the hand, a gentle thud, a growing pool of red.

The job is done.

Half a mile away, Adira watches in horror as she sees the queen order her henchmen to kill her mother. Tears stream silently down Adira's cheeks, but she is surprisingly calm for a toddler.

Yet something strange happens. Rather than lying there, limp and lifeless as most corpses, Rose's body crumbles away, reduced to ashes until it disappears, dissolving, almost, into the air around it.

The queen narrows her eyes. All logic, all science defies that. Even with the little magic she knows of, well, even crumbling bodies are a stretch. She could get someone to look into it, perhaps. But if it is magic, they will never find out, especially because the Cardens are hidden now. It would be futile to search—a waste of time and money and effort. Besides, she has what she came to get—the little girl. Adira will never suspect a thing—she is only five; she'll forget.

So, turning around, she walks to the contraption, gets in, and glides silently away. Everything is going as planned. Her revolution has just started.

***

"Why did you show me that? I thought you were one of them," Adira says quietly to Yukimura.

The guard had taken her up a hill near the cottage where Rose and Adira lived, knowing the queen's plans.

"Adira," she says gruffly, but still gentler than before, "My name is Yukimura, and I served the Cardens, the most prominent magical family until they were cast out. I was forced to serve the queen and her new age of 'science'—if you can even call her vicious methods 'science,'" she mutters as an afterthought.

"But I will always be loyal to the Cardens, to your family. And you deserve to know, no matter how young you are. I am on your side, no matter what," she finishes, looking sympathetically at Adi.

The little girl is silent. She stares at the place where her mother died. Then she turns to Yukimura once more, her intelligent violet eyes glistening like a cat's in the dark, and says, "Take me to wherever the queen wanted you to."

Yukimura nods without a word, and the two walk to one of the strange contraptions.

It's time for Adira to make a new life. So, weighed down by sadness and wisdom and emptiness beyond her years that can only come from an experience like this, they travel to her new home.

***

Finally, my time is coming, thinks the queen.

For when the little girl looks back upon the evening, all she will remember is hazy violet and falling stars and pure, black, stifling nothing.

She won't remember the people lying on the ground or the powerful feeling of sparks and energy running up and down her spine. She won't remember her bold escapade to the moon-cursed trees or her near freedom. And she won't remember the crumbling white body of her dead mother.

Yukimura will have given Adira the memory-swiping drink by now. She will recall nothing of tonight, nothing of her old life or her waste-of-space mother—nothing but my kindness. She will receive me with mercy. She will trust me, the perfect mother, me, the perfect queen! And then, the experiments can begin.

Or so the queen thinks.

Because the little girl with the light-up shoes just saw something she will never forget. And that one memory is enough to destroy everything the queen has worked for.

The queen should watch out. The family she worked so hard to keep out, the magic she tried so hard to destroy for power and revenge—they are all coming back, compressed in one little girl with amethyst eyes and blazing silver energy and the power of the gods.

Adding Tension

Kristi Wright mentored Natalie Sharp through a revision focused on adding tension in Natalie's humorous story, *The Skating Goat*.

Dear Reader,

Natalie Sharp's *The Skating Goat* is the clever and highly entertaining tale about a circus goat who desperately wants to learn how to skateboard. Natalie made wonderful use of both point of view and sensory detail. Through her tight point of view, I never once questioned that Frisk was a goat, and her sensory detail brought the setting to life and furthered the action.

We decided on a revision focus of adding tension. Tension hooks the reader and makes the story impossible to put down. We talked about upping the tension by adding at least one more hurdle to Frisk's adventure and by including more of Frisk's emotional reaction to her hurdles.

Generally, writers insert hurdles or tension in between the main character and their goal. In *The Skating Goat*, Frisk's goal is to skate at the skate park. Therefore, a huge opportunity for adding tension was when Frisk escaped from the circus and worked her way across the street to the park. Natalie added tension by having a car almost hit Frisk. She then revealed the strong reaction by both Frisk and the driver to this tense moment.

One strategy we used to brainstorm new opportunities for tension in *The Skating Goat* was to play a game called "Fortunately, Unfortunately." In this game, one person comes up with a fortunate event for the story and then another person builds on that with an unfortunate event. By alternating fortunate and unfortunate events, you can brainstorm possible hurdles (which create tension) for your story.

It was such a pleasure to work with Natalie Sharp. I'm thrilled that you will read her creative and hilarious tale about an intrepid and fun-loving goat.

I hope you will find many opportunities to add tension into your own stories in the future!

Kristi Wright

Kristi Wright is the author of the middle-grade, futuristic *Basker Twins in the 31st Century* series. She writes both middle-grade novels and picture books. In addition to her futuristic novels, she loves to write stories that are magical or whimsical. She conducts writers' workshops at elementary and middle schools that focus on sensory detail and a strong character point of view. She is an Assistant Regional Advisor for the Society of Children's Book Writers and Illustrators. A Young Inklings mentor, she lives and writes in Santa Clara, California.

Natalie Sharp

Natalie is ten years old and heading into fifth grade. In addition to writing, she loves to draw, read, play computer games, and create iMovies. She especially likes to draw horses. Some of her favorite books include the *Warrior Series* by Erin Hunter and *Harry Potter* by J. K. Rowling. If she could go anywhere in the world, Natalie would go to France, but honestly, she would prefer to visit her own imaginary world, which, of course, would be called, "Natalie World." Natalie lives in Mountain View, California, with her parents, her younger sister, Isabel, and her Beta Fish, Maxy III. She would like to give special thanks to Goat Simulator (her almost-favorite video game) for inspiring her to write *The Skating Goat* and to Undertale (her favorite video game) where she got the name "Frisk" for her main character.

Kristi Wright: How did you come up with the idea for *The Skating Goat* and what's your favorite part?

> **Natalie Sharp:** Before I wrote *The Skating Goat*, I was playing Goat Simulator, so that was on my mind. My favorite part of the story is when the car almost hits Frisk as she crosses the street. I like that the driver was surprised, and he stopped because there was a goat crossing the street!

Q: What's your favorite part of writing?

> **A:** I like that you can write about anything you want, and you don't need a computer or a fancy typewriter. You just need

your imagination and the knowledge of how to write.

Q: How was it revising _The Skating Goat_? Did the idea of adding tension make sense? Can you use this in future writing?

> **A:** Well, revising was just like writing except it was shorter. I think adding tension makes the story more exciting because there are more interesting things.

Q: What advice do you have for other Inklings who may not want to revise?

> **A:** While you don't have to revise, it will make it a little better, and you will be able to change your mistakes.

Q: Are you working on a new story?

> **A:** Yes, my new story is called _Wild Pearl_. It's about a cat. I'm also writing and drawing a comic book called _Hunter into Hunted_.

Q: Do you ever feel stuck in writing? What do you do?

> **A:** Yeah, that happens a lot. It's useful to take a break. You'll have a lot of inspiration during that time. Then you can get back into it.

Q: Do you have any advice about writing?

> **A:** Write about what you like because you know about that, and you might like writing it. I like cats so I write about cats, and I also like drawing so I make comic books. Also, most of the main characters in my stories are girls. In fact, in all the stories I've written, the main character is a girl.

The Skating Goat

by

Natalie Sharp

Frisk stuck her head in between the bars and pulled it out quickly as a Human walked by. She was planning to escape the circus. Frisk was a gray goat with trouble to spare and a taste for adventure. She lived in the almost-middle of the circus in a small field with five other goats. They barely moved or talked at all. Frisk, on the other hand, was the only goat that liked to run, so Humans came to the "goat pen" to look at only her. The only thing that Frisk liked to do was look. And run.

Every day, she would climb onto a big rock in the corner of her pen and stare at the skate park. Frisk was interested in the Humans riding on conveniently-shaped boards with wheels and the sloped slippery ground that they rode on. No matter how much Frisk *didn't* stare at the skate park, she would never love it less. So today she was planning to escape the boring, but clean, pen and try to learn to skate. She would do it at the skate park, of course.

It was getting dark and fewer Humans were in sight. This was the only time the circus was quiet and free from Humans, so Frisk planned

her escape then. The only hard part was getting over the fence. It was twice as high as Frisk, and only her horns could peek over the top if she tried climbing.

A single cricket chirped in the distance. A single Human and its kids walked by. A single moon glowed in the sky. A single light bulb went off in Frisk's head. If she could jump onto the big rock, she could jump over the fence! They were about the same height. Frisk backed up to get a running start. Once she was some distance away, she ran…and jumped! It was almost the highest she had ever jumped! Actually, it *was* the highest she had ever jumped! That was because she *really* wanted to see the skate park.

Frisk looked back at her "friends." They were sleeping like logs. Not surprising. Frisk made a face at them (or tried to, since she is a goat, and they don't make faces) and carried on.

A max of ten Humans were roaming the streets. Frisk observed this after she found her way out of the circus gates. She had to squeeze through them and past the ticket-taking Human, but seeing that the ticket-taking Human wasn't paying attention, Frisk knocked down the gates and trotted over them.

When she reached the parking lot, she could see the skate park more clearly. It was to her left, and a small segment of a street led there. Frisk's loud hooves banged on the road as she ran toward the skate park. Frisk was free! Now she could ride on those boards and almost fly through the air on the light-blue slopes.

She faltered as a loud sound like very low-pitched "baas" reached her small ears when she was halfway across the street. What was it? Frisk peeked over. One thought flashed through her mind as a red blur came closer and closer. *It's a car!* Before Frisk could even think another thought, it squealed to a stop.

The car was very close to her. The Human inside it looked surprised. Frisk looked surprised, too, and a litt e afraid—her ears were straight up, her eyes were round as watermelons (her favorite snack), and she let out a tiny squeak. She was g ad the car didn't crush her.

Frisk quickly crossed the street.

Frisk had heard stories about cars: Cars could be different colors, and they were very hard to describe. It was a small house with huge wheels—half the size of Frisk—on the bottom. They had windows on all sides and hidden doors. A parking lot stored the cars while the Humans did other stuff, like go to the circus.

That was all Frisk could describe of cars since she didn't know much else. Frisk had heard stories of cars crushing Humans and… goats! That part she hated, so Frisk mostly stayed away from cars. That's why she was scared.

Frisk's excitement returned as she again stared at the skate park. It was bigger than she thought it would be. But Frisk stopped short as she realized there was no way in. A big slope stretched up in front of her, cyan and slippery, like the other slopes she had seen from her rock. It blocked her way.

Wait! Frisk thought. *I can just run up the slope! I know the skate park must be on the other side.*

Frisk summoned up her bravery. She walked back a few paces to get a running start like back at the circus. And she ran forward and tried to run up the slope. The only problem was that Frisk just slid back down and gave up immediately. She is not a goat who keeps trying.

But she *did* keep trying to find a way to get to the skate park. So

she went around the big slope…but found *another* slope! This time, it was made of wood. Frisk started up the slope and found it wasn't slippery or *slope-ey* like the other one. It was easy to walk up. To Frisk's delight, she saw only two Humans. And they were just talking together, not paying attention to Frisk.

There were two boards next to the Humans. Frisk finally got to see one up close! She sneaked around the Humans and stepped onto one of the boards. But Frisk accidentally rolled backward and knocked over the female Human. A second later, the Human stood up and ran out of sight, screaming. It must be non-normal for goats to be out of their pens.

Frisk thought she heard the female Human scream, "Isn't that the goat from the circus?"

The male Human did nothing, so Frisk just hobbled over to the actual slopes.

She sped up on her board and had fun twisting and turning on the slopes. Frisk skated the whole night, happy as can be! But there was a time when she was racing too fast—she was just a gray-and-brown blur swarming around the skate park. But that was too fast, so she accidentally raced off the highest slope and flew through the air. She landed on the street that led to the skate park. Frisk groaned and got up. Skating wasn't as safe as she thought it was. She limped over to the sidewalk so that no cars would run over her while her side was recovering.

Frisk looked longingly at the skate park. Even if it wasn't safe, it was extremely fun. But it was getting light, and the sky was growing pink. Frisk followed the road back to the circus, where she crashed through the gates again and found her pen.

Frisk decided that she would sleep for the whole day because she was *tired!* She also decided she would do this every night. That would mean she would sleep like a log like her friends…but Frisk didn't care about that. Skating was more fun than doing tricks—even if the Humans depended on her for entertainment.

So the next night, she stole a skateboard and stuffed it in a big crack in the side of one of the slopes so she would always know where it was, and no one else would steal it. She even dipped her hoof in mud and slapped it on the skateboard—her signature—so everyone would know it was hers.

That was day one of Frisk being nocturnal—sleeping in the daytime, skating in the nighttime.

Setting Up the Story

Dear Reader,

Kai's First Kiss by Anabel Orozco is a delightful story with a likable main character who encounters a unique problem. In Anabel's revision, we focused on setting up the beginning. Anabel developed an excellent problem in the middle of her story, so I wanted to feel more connected to the story in the beginning. I asked Anabel to consider adding details at the beginning of her story to hook readers in.

Writers play with beginning lines to find one that best draws readers into the story. Writers also introduce the basics in the beginning: who, what, when, and where. Anabel successfully added these details to her beginning in order to ground the reader in the world of her story.

Anabel found the revision process challenging but fulfilling. Once she revised one sentence, she discovered she needed to go through the story to make sure the story made sense. She ended up making small adjustments throughout her story, and the result is truly wonderful!

Jena Brigantino

Jena Brigantino grew up playing outdoors in California where she dreamed up stories featuring animals. She wishes she could have participated in an Inklings program as a child. As Managing Director of SYI, she strives to extend the opportunity to as many children as possible. Jena holds a BA in Creative Arts with a minor in Education from San Jose State University. In her spare time, Jena enjoys spending time with her big Italian family where memorable stories are constantly shared...loudly!

Anabel Orozco

Anabel wrote this story in 2016. Her birthday is February sixth, and she was born in 2009. She does gymnastics and swimming. She's really interested in science and history—especially the lives of Beethoven and Alexander Hamilton. She's very curious about everything and asks lots of questions, like "who, what, where, why, when."

Jena Brigantino: How did you come up with the idea for *Kai's First Kiss?*

> **Anabel Orozco:** I got the idea from a dream, a book, and my brother.

Q: How did you revise your story? What was most helpful?

> **A:** I read it out loud and found things I wanted to change. Then I found more things that needed to be changed afterward. If you change the first sentence, you have to change the second sentence and more sentences, so the story makes sense. I also thought of what my teacher said about stories needing a problem that makes sense and a beginning, middle, and end.

Q: What advice do you have for other Inklings who are about to write stories?

> **A:** I'd tell them to finish the story all the way to the end. Make sure your story has a beginning, middle, and an end. The

problem should be in the middle and a solution that makes sense should be at the end.

Q: What are you writing now?

A: In school, we're writing a story about water, so I thought that I could write a story about Kai or a create a new character. I also started writing in a travel journal on my trip to the Grand Canyon.

Kai's First Kiss

by

Anabel Orozco

Once upon a time, there was a boy named Kai, who was slow and not very smart. He was seventeen years old. He had a BFF named Ricardo. They did lots of things together, like going into the forest to climb trees and to catch wild animals. They spoke in English, and many of their friends didn't understand them because they didn't speak this language.

Kai knew a girl named Steffany because she was in his science class. She was very pretty, and she had black hair and blue eyes.

Kai wanted to give Steffany a kiss because she was pretty, and he liked people with black hair and blue eyes. He thought if he bought her a necklace, then she would like him and give him a kiss. So he asked Ricardo to help him by getting a $200 necklace for Steffany, but Ricardo said he was busy studying so he couldn't.

Kai started thinking about a different way that he could make Steffany like him, but he couldn't think of one. The next day, Kai asked Steffany what she would like. Steffany looked at him with her blue eyes, like she didn't care.

Kai asked Steffany, "Will you kiss me?"

She said, "Okay. But only if you give me the moon."

She didn't really want him to kiss her and she thought he'd never be able to give her the moon. Then Steffany turned her back on him and walked away with her friends.

That made Kai feel sad because he didn't know how to get the moon. It was time to go home. He started walking home, feeling lonely, walking with his head down and his arms loose, hanging down. He thought and thought about how to get the moon for Steffany. When he got home, it was night, and he saw a shadow of the moon on his feet.

Then he had an idea. "Maybe I could ask the moon if I could use his shadow."

The next night, he went and talked with the moon, and he asked the moon if he could use his shadow.

"Moon, will you make a shadow in my room tomorrow night?" asked Kai.

"Yes, of course," the moon said because he wanted to be nice.

The next day, when it was time to leave school and return home, Kai raced to Steffany and said, "Come to my house today. I have the moon."

Steffany thought he was lying. She had told Kai to get the moon because she thought it was impossible to get the moon, so he wouldn't be able to kiss her.

So she said, "Okay, take me to your house."

When Steffany arrived at his house and saw the shadow of the moon, she was surprised to see that he had gotten the moon for her.

Steffany really wanted the moon, so she said, "Okay, we'll kiss."

She didn't care if he was dumb or smart. She just wanted the moon.

Kai felt really happy. Kai wished Ricardo were there so Ricardo would say, "Oh gosh, I should've gotten that necklace for her."

Then they kissed.

Suddenly, Ricardo shoved the door open and said, "I've been looking everywhere for you. I got the necklace! And I wasted all my money on it."

Kai said, "I don't need it anymore."

"So I got this for nothing?" Ricardo asked.

"No, you can still put it on her," said Kai.

Ricardo gave the necklace to Kai. Kai tried to put it on Steffany, but Steffany didn't like it because it was gray and she hated gray.

Kai and Steffany kissed again. Ricardo was so surprised—he stood there with his mouth and eyes wide open. Then Ricardo fainted.

And Kai and Steffany lived happily ever after in "Future-Me World."

Show, Don't Tell

Sarah Rogers mentored Maya Lopez through a revision focused on showing detail in Maya's story, *A Journey to a New Land*.

Dear Reader,

As I read Maya's story, *A Journey to a New Land*, I was struck by what a deep thinker Catalina, the protagonist is. I like that her "mind drifts with the tide." One thing that stood out to me, though, was that Catalina mostly didn't engage with other characters. It was almost as though Catalina were floating through the events in a cloud of her thoughts, making this adventure story feel very dreamy.

In Maya's revision, I asked her to focus on "show, don't tell," a pretty common piece of writing advice—and one that's a little vague. More specifically, I wanted the character of Catalina to show us how she engages with the people around her.

In an earlier version of this story, Catalina says, "I put down my map and follow the others to see what the commotion is about." When she leaves the map room, she seems to be alone with the wind, the salty air, and the fog. Even though she says that she followed some people, she only notices the land because she hears a yell and her "eyes follow to where the finger is pointing." Here's what I wondered as I was reading:

- Where did all of the people go that Catalina said she was following? Is she far away from them now? Why?
- If there are people near her, how are the others moving? Are they running and pushing each other for a good view or walking in a calm line?
- How many people are on the ship? Are they all on deck to find out if they're near land, or does Catalina notice that some people are missing?
- If Catalina is near people, why doesn't she ask any of the others what they've seen? Do any of the others talk to each other? Or, does Catalina find it strange that no one is talking in this exciting moment?

It would be too much to answer all of those questions in a revision, but those are the kinds of details that help readers "see" the other people in the scene. It might help to imagine that you're writing a scene for a play or movie and need to include stage directions about what other characters are doing.

Feel free to play around with your choices. You'll find that different details produce different effects. Go with your gut, and don't be afraid to change your mind!

Sarah Rogers

Sarah Rogers is the Fiction Editor for *The Rumpus*, a reviewer for *Publishers Weekly*, and the author of the chapter book *Inevitable What*—a collection of poems on travel, ritual, and magical objects. For doodles, musings, and more of her work, visit sarahlynrogers.com

Maya Lopez

Maya is in seventh grade at Summit Denali. Her writing experience includes writing essays and narratives for school, as well as free writing and editing with some other writers she knows. She mostly writes fiction, fantasy, and poetry. Other than writing, Maya likes reading, knitting, and playing guitar and ukulele. Her dream job is to be an architectural engineer.

Sarah Rogers: How long have you been writing?

Maya Lopez: I started writing mixed-up fairy tales in the third grade and have kept on writing since then.

Q: What feels different about your story now that you've revised it?

A: The flow is better, the main character is easier to visualize, and the setting is easier to visualize as well.

Q: What was the most useful or interesting thing you learned from the experience of revising this story?

A: Learning that it is not always the big changes that are needed or are the most effective, but small edits and changes here and there can go a long way.

Q: What was your process for researching the historical details of this story, and are you planning to write any more historical fiction in the future?

> **A:** I did all of my research about this event beforehand so that I could pull details as I needed them. I would definitely like to write more historical fiction in the future.

Q: What are your favorite genres to read?

> **A:** I like to read pretty much everything except nonfiction. My favorite genres are historical fiction and realistic fiction.

A Journey to a New Land

by

Maya Lopez

We have been at sea for quite a while now; I have lost track of exactly how long. My mind drifts with the tide. I shake my head to bring myself back to the present. I stand over the map that I have made, looking over the plotted course, and then at my name in small print in the corner: "Catalina."

I am the ship's cartographer—it is my duty—and it is how I managed to get aboard this ship. Looking again at the map, I realize that we should have been able to have seen the coast days ago.

Have we taken a wrong turn? Has the thick fog been blocking the view of the coast all along? Have we gotten lost among the sameness of the salty blue-green-gray ocean? I fret over all of the possibilities of misfortune.

An excited call cuts through the silence and abruptly interrupts my thoughts. The next few moments are silent, and then this first call is followed by one, then two, and then many more yells of joy. The calls are not of any word in particular, but just pure yelps of happiness.

Is it an island? Or another ship? I ask myself, wondering what this disruption could be about.

I hear footsteps, one after the other. They pass by my door and continue toward the front of the ship. I put down my map and follow the others to see what the commotion is about.

As soon as I exit the map room, the wind whips through my hair, sending the long, dark strands astray. I follow my crewmates, their tall forms sprinting toward the front of the ship. The air is intoxicatingly strong with the smell of salt. I grip the smooth wooden railing and lean over it, squinting, trying to see through the thick fog. I hear my crewmates whispering among themselves, but I am unable to hear what they are saying. Their subdued behavior seems unusual in this moment of discomposure. Even though I have squinted and scanned all that I could, I still don't see anything. I start to turn around to return to the map room.

I guess it was a false alarm; nothing is new here, I think, disappointment eating at the hope of seeing something different among the striking similarity of the vast ocean's waves—the waves that we see and sail through each day.

Then I hear a yelp of excitement, and I see someone's finger pointing into the dark gray fog. I quickly turn around. *Maybe now there is something new out there.*

My eyes follow to where the finger is pointing, at an appearing shoreline. This shoreline had just appeared; only moments ago, I had been disappointed, my hopes diminished. But now, I am ecstatic with the idea of going somewhere new. This shoreline is all that I needed to wash away my worries of being lost in the boundless ocean. Cutting through the fog, I can see the coast of a mainland, along with the riches that we are in search of, appearing right before my eyes. This coast glitters like a sparkling diamond, the sand standing out against the dull, uniform ocean.

My crewmates holler out of excitement, but I cannot hear them, their words are lost to the wind. I see a few hugging each other, but even some look uncertain at the prospect of finally leaving the ship that we have been on for so long. I see people on their knees, heads bowed, hands clasped, praying to God, thanking him for his kindness. These last weeks haven't been easy ones. We had an enormous storm overtake us, and we were almost blown off course.

We sail forward, closer and closer to the shoreline, our dreams of riches becoming more of a reality. As we approach the shore, close enough to see it clearly, men rush forward with ropes thicker than both of my arms. Now, not only the shoreline, but a harbor, comes into view. The rough waves that we had to sail through are gone, replaced by glassy blue water, calmly lapping the sparkling sand.

The men throw the humongous anchor into the water, slowing the ship's movement to a gentle drift. Once the ship is secure, our leader, Hernán Cortés, along with his translator, carefully exit the ship. Everyone is armed in case the greeting goes badly. The air is thick and tense. Sitting, watching, and waiting. My crossbow is loaded, and I am ready to fire if given the command. If this greeting goes badly, then we will have gained a new enemy and will not be able to carry out our search for riches in this location, extending our journey.

A man dressed in fine clothes walks into the open. He wears robes of many colors, ranging from blood reds to shimmering golds. Based on his fine clothes and his confident posture, it is obvious that this man is the ruler. He walks up to Cortés. Meanwhile, aboard

the ship, it is so silent that the quietest whisper could be heard. In contrast to our silence, is the sound of the waves rolling onto the shore. Everyone is tense and ready to get Cortés back to safety if necessary. Cortés and the ruler exchange a few words. I am not able to hear what is said, for I am out of hearing range.

This greeting seems to go well, as Cortés tells us, "You may exit the ship, without weapons, for no enemy has been made. Welcome to Potonchan."

Everyone onboard the ship relaxes. My crewmates release their tensed shoulders and lower their weapons. I can practically feel their relief in the air. I unload my crossbow and stow it with the rest of the weapons onboard the ship.

We exit the ship, some pushing and shoving each other to reach solid ground, while others take their time. My feet set down on the soft and damp soil. I totter from side to side—my legs still accustomed to familiar rocking rhythms of the ship. I look around and notice that I am not the only one who is off-balance. My crewmates' legs shake, but, nevertheless, we stand tall as Cortés instructs us; his voice is commanding, calm, and even in tone.

"You are free to wander, but not far. You must be ready to carry out the defense plan if we are attacked. Go."

I wander near the harbor, and a bustling market catches my eye. I walk toward this busy area, and I see goods being exchanged. I catch a glimpse of a woman trading a length of cloth for a few pieces of meat. I see another pair trading two woven baskets for a shining silver and gold necklace. As I near the market, the smell of wholesome grains, ripe fruits, and fresh vegetables fills the air. The air is sweet and ripe, full of exotic scents that I can't even begin to name.

People are sitting behind mats that display the goods they have to trade and sell. Most of these sellers are women—their long, dark-brown hair framing their tan faces. Their clothing is simple and somewhat lacking decency for some. I see colorful woven cloth that takes the shape of pouches, mats, as well as many other purposes.

The next mat displays fresh green fruits. Their outer skin is a shade of dark green—so dark that it is almost black. I see a woman halving these fruits. On the inside, they are a light shade of green, somewhat tinged darker around their outer edges. They contain a light brown stone-like pit that the woman proceeds to remove. I watch as she scoops out their insides, which look soft, and they squish as she mixes them together. Cooked fruits, peeled fruits, and raw fruits—they fill the woman's mat and look fit for the king himself. Their ripe smell fills the air, making my mouth water.

I walk past the ripe fruits to the next mat, which displays woven baskets. The baskets range in shape from tall and skinny to short and round. One of these baskets even appears to be watertight. A woman is washing vegetables in the basket filled with water, and when she lifts up the basket, no watermarks appear on the mat.

The thing that catches my eye is neither fruits, nor cloth, nor baskets. What I see is a woman herding a flock of ducks. One of the ducks ruffles its soft feathers, reminding me of the ducks that I used to see with my younger sister.

Oh, how she loved to walk to the pond and watch the birds, I think wistfully, wishing my sister were beside me. *Maybe I'll try to buy one; I don't like traveling alone anyway.* I think.

Well, now for the interesting part—I have to let the woman know that I want to buy a duck, regardless of the language barrier. I

pull a thick, round golden coin out of my small leather bag, and this catches the woman's attention. I point at the coin in my hand, and then at one of the particularly colorful ducks, and then back at the coin in my hand. The woman tentatively takes the coin out my hand. All of a sudden, she puts it in the corner of her mouth, and proceeds to bite it! The woman makes a face and gives the coin back to me. I'mperplexed, but not ready to give up. Once more, I point at the coin, at the duck, and then back at the coin. The woman seems to understand what I want this time and clutches her ducks protectively. Feeling miffed, I walk away from the woman.

I mean, really! I work hard to earn that money, and first she tries to eat it, and then she flat-out refuses it! I continue walking through the market, seeing what goods others have.

As I continue my stroll through the market, it becomes harder and harder for me to walk forward because everyone—the Spanish and the natives—is heading in the opposite direction. They all seem to be rushing toward the same place. Wanting to find out what the commotion is about, I turn around and follow the majority. I am shoved about in the crowd, not being acknowledged by those around me. The crowd starts to turn out of the market and into the harbor. I am stuck in the middle of the crowd, following the people who are now sprinting and don't care who they run into. As I follow the crowd toward the harbor, I brush past the woman with the ducks; she is holding as many ducks as she can in her arms—about five—while the rest follow faithfully at her heels. The woman turns her head, and when she sees me, she clutches her ducks protectively and walks on, but faster now. Once we are at the harbor, I make my way toward my crewmates; they seem to be waiting for something, and very impatient as well. Conversation rustles through the crowd.

"What is going on?" I ask the crewmember standing next to me.

"Catalina! Be quiet! Cortés has an announcement to make!" yells my crewmate.

My face turns red with embarrassment. Well, at least now I know what is going on. The murmurings and conversations are hushed, as a silence falls over the crowd. Cortés is standing beside his translator, next to whom stands the ruler of Potonchan.

Cortés clears his throat before speaking, "The ruler has asked that we leave—neither as allies nor as enemies." The ruler of Potonchan translates this message for the natives.

Angry yells erupt from my crewmates around me.

"What about the riches that we came in search of?" one shouts.

"Was this journey all for nothing?" yells another.

The natives hear the anger in their voices, even though our different tongues separate us. They begin to respond with angry shouts of their own. None of the crew can understand what is being yelled, as they continue yelling. Both sides sound equally hostile and flustered. Both sides seem offended that the other side is angry at them. They stand on the tips of their toes, making themselves larger and larger with their anger. I try to take up as little space as possible. I put my hands over my ears, trying to block out the noise. Even though my hands are over my ears, I can hear the muffled yells, getting louder and angrier. I squeeze my eyes shut, thinking that maybe if I think hard enough, this will all be a dream. I slowly open one eye. Nope, not a dream. I'm stuck in the middle of a chaotic crowd, and who knows how much longer this will go on. I am thrown around by the jostling of my angry crewmates.

One agonizing minute passes, then two—each passing minute is complete chaos.

Finally, a booming voice cuts through the yells, "ENOUGH!" shouts Cortés, his face stressed and red as a tomato.

A silence settles back over the crowd, and Cortés addresses the crew in a shaky voice. "This journey is not for nothing; we will make multiple stops and find our riches elsewhere."

Cortés then has a quick exchange with the ruler of Potonchan through his translator, who then translates the message for both the crew and the natives. "We will leave this city peacefully; neither as allies nor enemies. We will spare this city from war, and we will find our riches elsewhere. Prepare the ships to leave now."

Our crew jumps into action. Goods purchased and gifts received are loaded onto the ship by our strongest warriors and deckhands. I pick my way across the worn wooden deck, weaving around men carrying a box of vegetables and around men carrying boxes of precious gold and gems.

I find the map room, and I push open the wooden door, and when it swings shut behind me, the noise on the deck and the chattering of the natives—called Mayans—quiets. A calm spreads throughout the room as I sit down in my chair. I pick up the map that I made and look at its carefully plotted course, starting in Spain and ending in Potonchan. Our short time in Potonchan has opened my eyes to a new place. A new civilization.

I realize why we were asked to leave. If we had become allies, Potonchan would be expected to give men and weapons. If they were enemies, a war could have started. A war could have destroyed the bustling little town.

Then I continue thinking. *If a small war could have destroyed Potonchan, a large one could put an end to the world as we know it. Peace is important. Without peace, our world would be completely different.* I begin deliberately plotting our next course. Our journey and search for riches will continue—to a new civilization, to a new world.

Dialogue

Kavita Singh mentored Sahana Srinivasan through a revision focused on dialogue in Sahana's story, *The Mystery of the Disappearing Pets.*

Dear Reader,

If you're a lover of animals like I am, then *The Mystery of the Disappearing Pets* is guaranteed enjoyment! Sahana did a great job creating action and adventure, mystery and wonder, elements of magic, and an overall fun plotline that will have you reading until the end. It was my pleasure to revise her story, and I hope she continues to write and create even more wonderful stories to share.

In my revision of Sahana's story, I asked her to focus on dialogue. With so many exciting characters involved in the story's twists and turns, it's always important to help every character have their voice. Some characters are important throughout, others come in at certain points, and still others may not even speak at all. Dialogue is an important element of storytelling and helps readers step into the story through the people (and animals!) that are involved in it.

When revising, focusing on dialogue is an important way to start. After all, the words people say is a concept that writers of all ages can understand. How do you make your character more alive? Start with a single passage or event in a story. In that moment, are they fearful, thoughtful, proud? How would they feel about the words they're about to say? Perhaps they'll be yelled at, or perhaps it's some much-needed encouragement from a friend. These are great questions to ask and explore. Try putting yourself in your character's shoes while you are writing. And it doesn't just have to be on the page, either—you can act out your characters, draw them, and engage with them in other creative ways. I promise you, it's sure to help the characters come alive.

Kavita Singh

Kavita Singh is a writer and is excited to mentor this year as a part of Inklings. She's worked at several tech companies, and, in her free time, enjoys cooking, dancing, rock climbing, movies, long walks, and (of course!) writing. She enjoys stories of every kind and hopes that classic rock, comics, and video games could one day be considered fine art.

Sahana Srinivasan

Sahana is in second grade at Murdock Portal Elementary School. She enjoys reading, swimming, and going on hikes. She loves animals and wants to become a veterinarian when she grows up. Her favorite book series is the *Magic Tree House* series, and her favorite animal is a peregrine falcon because it is the fastest living creature. When she grows up, she would like to write fantasy stories and stories with animal characters.

Kavita Singh: What changed the most in your story when you did your revision?

> **Sahana Srinivasan:** The first part of the story, once they get their new pet, describing where they live and stuff like that. And also when they went to the vet, I added description.

Q: Who is your favorite character in *The Mystery of the Disappearing Pets?*

> **A:** I like all the characters, but my favorite is Helen. She was the one who chose Fluffy, and Fluffy helped them find the leprechaun, and the leprechaun helped them find their pets. And my second favorite is Fluffy, followed by Penny, and then John.

Q: How do you come up with your ideas?

A: An author came to our school, and he asked us to start a story. He gave us story options, and then the whole group started a story, and I took that and added more because I really wanted a story about a leprechaun.

Q: What do you enjoy most about writing?

A: Writing the story first on paper. I usually do very short stories, and, at my school, we have to write a story every day. If you want, you can continue a story that you wrote in the past; I had one about a farmer where a thief steals the pets after Christmas.

The Mystery of the Disappearing Pets

by

Sahana Srinivasan

Chapter One—The Dog

I want a rooster!" wailed Penny. Penny was a ten-year-old girl in fifth grade.

"No, of course not! A rooster isn't a proper pet. What about a pig?" asked her brother John. John was seventeen and was in the last year of high school.

"No," said their mother firmly. "A pig is too messy, and a rooster is too loud," she explained.

Their mother, Lilly, was a doctor who treated sick children and their dad, Alan, was a scientist who studied plants.

"Let's get a dog," said Helen, speaking up after some silence. Helen was thirteen years old and was in middle school.

It was going to be Penny's birthday next week, and she was allowed to choose one pet as a birthday present. The other children were helping her choose a new pet.

"That's a good idea if Penny is okay with it," said their dad, remembering that it was Penny's gift. "A dog would be a lot of fun to play with. Also, we can take him for walks, and that'll be good exercise for all of us," he said.

They already had a cat named Daisy, a bird named Tweet, a rabbit named Hoppity, and a squirrel named Scamper. The family loved their pets, and their home resembled a small zoo. They lived in a two-story house on a peaceful, tree-lined street with nice neighbors. They had a huge, beautiful backyard with lots of flowering bushes and fruit trees. The children spent a lot of time outdoors in the garden playing with their animal friends.

Later, the family got into their car and drove to the pet store. Soon they arrived at the pet store; there were many animals—cats, fish, hamsters, birds, dogs, and horses. Since the family had already decided they wanted a dog, they went straight to the section where the dogs were kept. There were many kinds of dogs of different colors. There were greyhounds, Labradors, retrievers, poodles, huskies, collies and pugs.

Suddenly, Helen spotted a golden retriever with thick brown fur, long brown ears, and clear blue eyes. She wanted the dog as soon as she saw it.

"Look, over there, John and Penny!" she said, pointing excitedly in the direction of the dog.

John and Penny turned to look where Helen pointed. They too loved the dog as soon as they spotted it.

"Can we please, please have that dog?" Penny asked her parents, pointing to the dog.

"Of course you can," said their dad.

The card in front of the dog's cage said that he was ten months old, two feet long, twenty-five pounds, and cost $100. They paid for the dog and walked out of the building with Lilly carrying the dog in her arms. The children were all very excited to be taking home their newest pet.

"What are we going to name him?" asked their mom, walking toward the car.

"I think his name should be Bundle because he looks like a cute, brown bundle," said John.

"I think we should name him Brown," said Penny.

"No, no!" interrupted Helen. "I think I have the best name for him," she said. "I think his name should be Fluffy—if Penny agrees."

Everyone, including Penny, loved the name and agreed immediately. They happily returned to their house with their new pet dog. What fun they were going to have with Fluffy!

Chapter Two—Petnapped

That night, their other pets greeted the newest member of the family. At dinner time, Lilly reminded everyone that they needed to take the pets to the vet for their regular checkup the next morning. John offered to take the pets to the vet since it was his summer break. Penny and Helen said they would go with him too since they were also on their summer break. Their parents agreed to this plan and said that they could leave after their breakfast at 9:00 a.m. Their mom offered to make them a picnic lunch, so they could spend some time at the park on their way back home.

Helen used her old sewing basket and her old camping

blanket to make a nice, comfortable bed for Fluffy. She put the basket in Penny's room for Fluffy. Fluffy was curious and excited about his new home and friends. The children went to sleep happily dreaming about the next day.

The next day was warm, sunny, and beautiful. John took Hoppity the rabbit in her cage. Penny took Tweet on her shoulder and walked Fluffy. Helen took Daisy and Scamper. They started walking along the street toward the vet's office.

"I love the long, warm days!" said Penny. She enjoyed not having to wake up early for school and not having to do homework.

"I have an idea! Let's go to our secret hideout after seeing the vet. It's been a while since we were there," said Helen.

The children agreed and walked into the pet hospital. After the vet had checked all their pets (including their newest one, Fluffy), the kids walked to their secret hideout, which was at the end of their neighborhood park where the grass grew tall. People didn't usually go beyond that corner. How the children discovered this corner is another story by itself. The secret hideout was a special place where the children came to play during days when they wanted to be on their own. Next to the secret hideout was a forest where they went hiking and sometimes had picnics.

When they reached the hideout, John said, "I am hungry!"

"Okay," said Helen. "Let's eat our picnic lunch now," she continued.

"We can play a game of cards after lunch," said Penny.

The children put down their pets, spread out the picnic blanket, and took out their food from their picnic baskets. They were in for a surprise when they unpacked their baskets! Their mom had packed a feast of their favorite foods! There were three sandwiches with their names on the wrapping. There were fresh fruit and a yummy salad as well. They also found a big homemade chocolate cake.

"What a treat!" said Penny, as she divided it up among everyone.

After they had finished feeding their pets, they played Uno. Helen turned around to get some water, and she was shocked to see that the pets had disappeared! All of their pets except Fluffy had vanished! John had been holding onto Fluffy's leash when he was playing cards.

Chapter Three—Plans and Packing

"Oh no! Our pets have disappeared!" cried Penny in alarm.

The children were in shock. They had just fed their pets a few minutes ago and couldn't understand how they suddenly disappeared.

"Let's be calm and not panic," said John, finally breaking the silence. "Let's use our five senses to see if we can figure out what happened to our pets," he said.

"I can't see any tracks because there is moss on the ground, and I did not notice anyone come near us," said Helen.

"I didn't hear a thing," said Penny, shaking her head. "All I heard was the wind blowing," she said.

"I didn't smell anything either," said John who was feeling quite confused.

The children looked around everywhere and still couldn't find their pets.

"What do we do now?" asked a worried Helen.

"The only thing we can do now is ask Mom and Dad if we can camp out here and look for our pets," said John after thinking hard.

It was evening by the time they decided to give up their search, and it was time to go home. The children went back home with gloomy faces and told their parents everything that had happened that day. Their parents were also very sad and frustrated.

"Mom, will you please let us camp out in the woods near the park? I have a feeling we may find them there. Maybe we can find them if we spend time looking for them by day as well as by night?" asked John.

With hopeful eyes, the other children also looked at their mom.

After thinking about it awhile, their mother frowned. "I am worried about you children being all alone," she said. "Then again, I believe John is big enough to take care of all of you, and you are all very responsible children. Take Fluffy with you as well. You know how dogs usually sense some things that we can't. Be careful and stay out of danger."

The next morning, John made a plan and told everyone what to do. Helen packed their sleeping bags, John packed their food, and Penny made a camp bed for Fluffy. Then they packed their clothes and camping things that they would need. They also carried flashlights, ropes, a hammer, nails, fishing poles, a box of matches, and their tent.

Chapter Four—The Leprechaun

The next day, they were ready to leave. Fluffy came with them. They reached the woods behind the park and looked for a good spot to pitch their tent. In the woods, there were colorful birds, orange foxes, and sleeping owls. The children loved the fresh air and the colorful flowers that were everywhere on the forest ground. They found just the right spot near the bank of a river. They spent the rest of the day putting up their tent and unpacking their things. Even Fluffy helped by gathering wood for the fire.

By the time the children finished setting up their tent, it was night time. It was close to midnight, and they were very tired. The next morning, Fluffy was the first to wake up. Penny woke up next, followed by Helen. John was the last to wake up.

"Helen, what day is it?" asked Penny.

"It's March 17," replied Helen, wondering why Penny was asking.

"Yay! Today is St. Patrick's Day! Maybe we'll spot a leprechaun. He might even bring us some luck," said Penny.

When they got out of their tent, Fluffy sniffed the air and seemed to smell something. He ran all the way across the bridge over the river. The children ran after him and could hardly keep up. He ran and ran and finally stopped in front of a big old oak tree. Suddenly, they heard little footsteps, and out of the bushes came a leprechaun! The children could not believe their eyes! He was about one foot tall, wearing a green top hat with a black belt around it. His suit was green and black, and each of his shoes had a four-leaf clover design. He looked like he came straight out of a storybook.

Helen wanted to run away in shock, but John stopped her. He knew that leprechauns didn't do any harm and were actually very funny and helpful. Penny just stared and could not move.

"Thank you for not running away from me!" said the leprechaun after a minute. "Most people are either afraid of me or want to hurt me. I am happy that you children did not do any of these. I know what you are looking for. I will give you a treasure map that will help you." Then he handed a treasure map to Penny and disappeared.

Chapter Five—The Wobbly Bridge

Everyone stayed silent for a minute. They still could not believe what had just happened.

Then John spoke, "I think we should use the map that the leprechaun gave us."

"No," said Penny, still feeling scared. "I think it might be dangerous because I have read that leprechauns are very sly and may sometimes trick you," she added.

"No," said Helen, "I agree with John. I don't think that leprechaun was dangerous. He looked like a friendly little fellow to me. Besides, he seemed to know what we were looking for. I also think we should follow the map," said Helen.

"Okay, if you both think this is a good idea, I am okay with it," said Penny, reluctantly.

"Okay, now that we've agreed to use this map, let's take a look," said John. He carefully held the treasure map in his hands, pointed, and said, "The map says to turn left at the oak tree and walk for two miles until you see a bridge across a river."

The children followed the directions on the map and reached the bank of a river and could see a bridge across it.

"Oh!" said Helen in panic as soon as she saw the bridge in front of her. "That bridge looks like it can hold only one person at a time, and it looks like it might fall any second!" she said with a worried look on her face.

"Wait, look at the river, it's a river of lava!" exclaimed Penny.

The river was indeed reddish orange in color with slow moving lava and fumes coming out of it.

"Oh, God! "We have a wobbly bridge and a lava river to cross!" said a scared Penny.

"Don't worry, we'll think of something," said John, trying to calm her.

They sat on the ground and tried to think of a way to get across. Suddenly, Helen had an idea. She explained it to the others.

"First, John crosses the bridge. Then Penny and Fluffy cross the bridge together since they are both light. Then I cross the river. We hold onto the railings of the bridge the entire time we're crossing, and we do not let go until we reach the end," said Helen. The children followed Helen's directions and finally made it across the lava river.

Chapter Six—The Dragons

"Come on, let's see what's next on the map," said Penny.

"The map says to go one mile east," said John.

They headed east and walked for a mile. Soon they arrived at a big door. "Let's push the door open," said John.

"No, we don't know what's behind it. It might be too dangerous," said Penny.

"Let's see what's in there—it might be our pets, after all!" said Helen, and she walked toward the door.

The children pushed the door open, and, to their surprise… they were face to face with a two-headed dragon!

"Wwwwhat should we do now???" Penny cried in fear.

No one answered her. John had already grabbed his water bottle from his backpack and was now flinging the water at the dragon's eyes. The water made the dragon's eyes burn, so it closed its eyes.

As soon as the dragon closed its eyes, John said, "Run away, quick! I will come as soon as I can!"

The children then ran past the two-headed dragon and through another door on the other side.

When the door was closed, Penny said "Whew! That was close! Thanks to John, we escaped!"

John joined the others. They found themselves in a large room with purple walls and pictures of dragons. It was a strange big room with no windows. In one corner, a big fire was burning in a fireplace.

Pointing to the farthest corner of the room, Helen said, "Look there, I see something."

They walked over to that corner of the room and found some type of machine sitting on a carpet. On the carpet, there was a card that read "Magic Carpet;" on the machine, there was a card that read "Time Machine." Penny spotted something shiny sitting on the seat of the time machine. She picked up the shiny object. It was a silvery piece of cloth, and the children found a note attached to it. The note said, "This cloak will allow the user to see things that cannot be seen by human eyes." After all of their adventures, the children were very happy to finally find what the leprechaun had left them.

Chapter Seven—The Gifts

John, Helen, and Penny were very excited to use their precious gifts in the search for their pets. They sat down in a semicircle to discuss what they should do next. After a lot of thinking, they agreed on a plan. They would use the time machine to go back to the day they lost their pets in the secret hideout. Then they would wear the silver cloak, which would allow them to see things that they couldn't see with their own eyes. After that, they would use the magic carpet to take them to whatever destination they needed to go to get their pets.

So, according to their plan, the children and Fluffy got into the time machine and went back to the day that they had lost their pets. They found themselves in the secret hideout again, and they quickly put the silver cloak around them. They could see themselves sitting down with their pets and having lunch. Then they noticed something that surprised them very much. They saw a tall, heavy man quietly hiding behind the bushes. They even knew who he was! He was Mr. Bill, the clerk at the post office! They knew him because he was their dad's friend's brother. He had once visited their home with his brother and had even said how amazing their pets were.

Mr. Bill first watched the children eat their lunch, and then he did something that the children were shocked to see. He waved something that looked like a wand at Hoppity the rabbit. The rabbit immediately turned into a little dandelion! Mr. Bill then did the same to each of the other pets, except Fluffy. He must have been afraid that the children would notice if he were to do the same to Fluffy because Fluffy was being held by John.

Once his job was done, he quickly left the area and walked back to the park. No wonder the children couldn't find the pets anywhere—they had been turned into dandelions! From within the cloak, they saw Mr. Bill return as soon as the children went home after giving up their search for their pets. He then turned all the pets back to their original forms and carried them home with him.

Chapter Eight—The Rescue

John, Helen, and Penny were shocked to learn how their pets were taken from them. They used the magic carpet to go home right away. They told their parents everything that had happened. Their parents called the police, and they all went to Mr. Bill's house, which was on a street with dirty homes on both sides. When Mr. Bill opened the door, he was surprised to see everyone. The police officer then explained why they were there and that he was going to be arrested for stealing the pets. Mr. Bill suddenly looked scared, and he admitted to stealing pets to sell them to pet stores for money. The police found out that Mr. Bill had been using magic to steal several pets, and he had many more pets in his house. They planned to return each one of them to their owners as soon as they could.

The children happily returned home with their pets after finally reuniting with them.

At dinner that night, the children's dad looked at them and said, "I'm so proud of you all, for you were very brave for your loved ones. You acted calm and wise in the face of danger and did not give up in spite of the many hard things you had to do. Your mom and I are the happiest people on earth now!"

John, Helen, and Penny were so thrilled to hear this from their parents, and they smiled happily at one another.

Detailed Descriptions

Briana Mitchell mentored Samantha Vargas through a revision focused on description in Samatha's story, *Dusty*.

Dear Reader,

Dusty is such a delightful and touching story of friendship. I was very excited to revise it with Samantha; I knew we'd have a lot of fun!

While we revised her story, we focused on adding in detailed description. She already had a wonderful knack for including lots of action in her story. She not only used action to move the plot forward, but she also used it as a tool to develop her characters. For instance, when the puppies first show up at Sarah's house, Samantha has them jumping around. That's a great detail! It tells us that the puppies are energetic and makes us wonder just what might happen in the coming pages.

I decided to work with Samantha on supplementing her natural understanding of action in a story with direct, detailed descriptions. In a story, action is like the cake and details are like frosting. Cake is really yummy by itself—but add some frosting to it, maybe make it look pretty with a few icing designs or some writing...and voila! You have a delicious masterpiece that nobody could resist. Take the example of the moment when the puppies arrive at Sarah's house. How much cuter and exciting would that moment be if we knew what they looked like? What if we knew what sounds they made? How did the four, first-time dog-sitters feel? You see? She already had a yummy cake, so we just put some frosting on it.

As she made her revisions, I asked her to think about the following things:

First: Details can help bring attention to the most important things in your story. Think about the biggest moments in your story. Is there a way to paint a clearer picture in your reader's head? What can you tell us about what your main character is experiencing in that moment? These moments are important; they're what your story is made of. So, we want to make sure your characters really pop out in your readers' minds.

Second: If you're wondering what kind of details to include, think about your own senses. How do you experience the world? Through your five senses: sight, hearing, touch, taste, and smell. Your character experiences the world the same way. So, ask yourself, what is your character is seeing, hearing, touching, tasting, and smelling? I'll add one more sense to that: feeling. Don't be afraid to tell us what emotions your character is feeling too!

Third: Pretend that there's no such thing as "overboard"!

Now is the time to add in as much detail as you want, change things, try out ideas you think might work. I'll be here to give you guidance if I think you've added too much or need to move in a different direction—that's my job! Your job is to write your heart out.

While revising, I also asked Samantha to keep in mind that I only highlighted areas in her story that could be improved. That doesn't mean I didn't notice all the amazing work she had already done! I was very impressed with her story from the beginning and am even more impressed with the final draft. Enjoy her beautiful writing!

Briana Mitchell

Briana Mitchell grew up in Portland, Oregon, where her favorite activities included reading, writing, and running into the forest to act out any freshly woven stories. Since moving to California and receiving her BA in Theatre and Spanish from Santa Clara University, not much has changed! Briana believes that stories are our greatest teachers. Whether it was a biography on Helen Keller, a journey across Middle Earth, or simply the latest and greatest from her father's surplus of bedtime stories, Briana's life was—and still is—consistently permeated and shaped by the stories she finds around her. Today, her work as a teacher, writer, and an actor is directly inspired by the power of a well-crafted story. Briana strives to share her passion for the written word with young writers and empower them to delve fearlessly into the stories they see unfolding in and around them every day.

Samantha Vargas

Samantha was born in 2008, and she was eight years old when she published this story, *Dusty*. She is currently in second grade at The Sammamish Montessori School. She has a black and white Havanese and has always enjoyed anything related to dogs. And she doesn't like pizza—unless she can cut it herself.

Briana Mitchell: How did you come up with the idea for *Dusty*?

Samantha Vargas: Well, I first thought of Dusty as an alley dog, and I really liked her, so I wanted to put the idea of Dusty into an award-winning book. In fact, she was a gray Havanese with the same personality, but she just didn't have an owner. In this story she's transformed from an alley dog to a pampered pooch!

Q: How do you think your story has changed throughout this process?

A: I think it's better because there's a lot of pizza jokes! I don't like pizza, but I like making jokes about it. I also think it's better because the editor helped me, and I liked that I talked more about Spike.

Q: What do you think you learned?

A: Be kind to dogs! I also learned that Dusty is really cute. I learned that writing is not always easy because you have to go through edit after edit after edit.

Q: Do you feel like the edits made your story stronger?

A: Yes!

Q: If you had to give advice to someone who was going to do this process next year, what would you tell them?

A: Add a lot of detail, and make sure you have a good story with a strong plot.

Q: Is there anything else you're writing right now?

A: *Dusty 2.*

Q: Is there anything else you'd like to say about your experience with the Inklings Book Contest?

A: Oh yeah! I liked writing it, and I'd like to say thank you to my teacher, Mrs. Long, for telling me about the contest.

Dusty

by
Samantha Vargas

It was a beautiful sunny day, and Sarah Anderson had just finished second grade. It was finally summer break, and Sarah was excited, except for one thing. She wished Spike, her dog, had been there. He used to lick her every time she got in the car after school. He wouldn't stop until they got home. Sarah loved how his wet, pink tongue touched her face and his curly brown hair touched her skin and his wet nose was always in her face. No matter what, his long and thin tail would always be wagging. But he had passed away in December.

She wished for another dog, but she didn't have enough money to adopt one. She didn't even have enough to get a toy one. Sarah came up with an idea to get some money. She needed mom to approve.

All summer, she would dog sit the neighborhood dogs! Lots of people in her neighborhood had dogs. Her mom approved but her dad did not. Her dad said that he couldn't let his daughter stay at home and babysit dogs. It could be dangerous. What if one of them

bit her!

Sarah said she would buy them pizza to eat for dinner," after she babysat the puppies. Dad could tell that she was serious because Sarah did not like pizza and buying it for dinner with her own money meant she was very serious. Dad said yes because he wanted his daughter to be happy no matter what, and he could tell that she would be happy babysitting puppies.

Her mom and dad helped her put out an advertisement. One neighbor, Mr. Yip, responded. He needed a dog sitter for his five puppies.

That was a lot of dogs.

Sarah's mom and dad said she would need help.

"I'm afraid we cannot let you dog sit," said Mom. "Not by yourself."

"I don't need help," said Sarah.

"No, no," said Mom. "Your friends must help you."

Sarah rushed to the phone and called her best friends, Larry, Elizabeth, and Ethan.

The next day, as Mom and Dad left for work, her friends arrived.

As soon as he stepped into the house, Ethan—a happy, black-haired boy—asked, "Where are the puppies?"

Ding Dong! The doorbell rang. Sarah opened the door and was startled to see five playful puppies eating the pizza she had ordered.

"That's my pizza!" she said.

"*This* is your pizza," said Mr. Yip, handing her another pizza box.

She looked inside to check if he was tricking her. He wasn't.

"I thought I'd buy my puppies some dog pizza for lunch," said

Mr. Yip. The puppies finished their pizza quickly and then ran all over the house. They jumped on the rug and on Sarah's couch, too. One was even messing with the refrigerator! Another one was pooping on the rug!

"We have to clean that up," said Sarah, and they did.

"Does this answer your question, Ethan?" asked Elizabeth, who always wore her long, brown hair in a ponytail. She was holding onto the top of the couch, avoiding a small puppy that was trying to lick her face. She had just finished cleaning up the poop on the rug.

"Yes," said Ethan, who was running around the house, avoiding several puppies that were chasing him.

Mr. Yip, the owner of the puppies, called out, "Good luck!" and left.

"Why does he have so many puppies?" asked Larry, an outgoing boy with green-dyed hair and green eyes.

"I have no idea," said Sarah.

After the puppies had explored the whole house, they fell asleep. So did Sarah and her friends.

***

Later that day, Sarah and her friends walked the dogs to the lake.

Elizabeth said, "I really like this dachshund."

Sarah took a peek at the puppy's collar. "Her name is Ginger," she said.

All of a sudden, the puppies ran to the side of the lake, barking happily. There was a small boat tied to the pier. Some puppies tried to jump in.

"They want to play in the boat!" said Sarah, enthusiastically.

Sarah's friends could tell that she wanted to go in the boat. Only one puppy did not want to go near the water. Sarah saw that this puppy's name was Dusty. She was a cute Havanese with gray hair and a diamond-studded collar. Her tail was long, and it curled up instead of down. She had a black nose, and her eyes looked like a dream.

"Hello, Dusty," said Sarah. Never in her life had she seen a gray Havanese. Mr. Yip was very lucky to have found her. Sarah knew she could never afford a dog like this.

The other puppies were already playing in the little boat; they had climbed in with Elizabeth, Ethan, and Larry. There was a chain on the boat that stretched to the dock so that the boat wouldn't go floating off by itself. Sarah picked up Dusty and climbed into the boat.

They were playing happily for a while, when suddenly, it began to rain.

Sarah and her friends tried to gather up the puppies, but they scampered everywhere. Then, lightning struck the chain, and the boat started to float away—before everyone got out! The puppies were yelping and barking because they were wet and afraid.

"Don't worry," said Larry. He tried to paddle with his hands toward the shore.

"But the pups are out of control," said Ethan.

Dusty was shivering in the corner. Ginger was jumping but not yelping. She looked like she enjoyed the rain. Another bolt of lightning hit the water and shook the boat. Dusty fell out. She yelped and was sinking into the water.

Sarah screamed, "We have to save her!" Without thinking, she jumped into the water and swam after Dusty. Dusty's yelping made it easy for Sarah to find her. She caught the puppy and got back into the boat. She felt very happy when she touched Dusty's wet, cold, gray hair.

While this was happening, Ethan found oars under a tarp in the boat. They rowed back to shore. Sarah was hugging the wet puppy. Dusty licked Sarah on the nose.

When Mr. Yip came to pick up his puppies, Sarah told him the whole story.

"I'm so sorry about the accident," Sarah said.

"I'm glad no one was hurt," he said.

Then he knelt down and petted Dusty. He looked into her eyes and saw a reflection. Dusty was looking at Sarah with love.

"You know what?" he said. "I have a lot of puppies. Maybe you can take care of Dusty for me if your parents approve."

Sarah was delighted. "Thank you!" she yelled.

Mr. Yip took his other puppies and went home. Sarah and Dusty had a wonderful summer vacation together. Sarah taught Dusty how to swim so that they could go to the waterpark together. They even played in the neighborhood park and sat in a chair. And Sarah bought Dusty a dog pizza. Sarah and Dusty couldn't wait for next summer vacation.

Foreshadowing

Dear Reader,

I was immediately mesmerized by Ben's story, *Whale Watching Past Westerndon*. It's a wonderfully whimsical whale of a tale! Ben has written a funny, enchanting, and creative fantasy jam-packed with talking birds, magical orange trees, a mysterious boy, and a pickle whale.

Ben's story already had so many interesting aspects that, to me, appeared as metaphors or as potential foreshadowing elements. I thought this would be an excellent opportunity to develop those scenes and to add to the intrigue of the story, so I chose foreshadowing as our revision focus.

Foreshadowing is a literary device that an author uses to give clues about events that will happen later in the story. For example, writers use foreshadowing to lead up to a story's twist. Mystery writers use foreshadowing to leave subtle clues for the reader, without giving away too much. But all kinds of stories can have foreshadowing—to use as metaphors or as information that is important to the story's plot.

Foreshadowing clues are often subtle, quietly slipped in by the sly writer; sometimes the reader is surprised at the end of the story and realizes only later how the foreshadowing pieces fit together—like a puzzle! And sometimes the foreshadowing is more obvious, giving the reader a sense of anticipation of what's to come. If you want to include foreshadowing in your story, it takes a little extra planning, but it's great fun!

Ben's story already employed several foreshadowing elements, but they were not yet developed. In fact, Ben was surprised and excited to learn how we could turn several aspects of his existing narrative into foreshadowing devices. Ben's descriptive imagery was perfect for introducing this type of storytelling. We just needed to play up what he already had and to add in a bit more narrative to make the story more robust.

In Ben's original version, the mother is haphazardly driving a purple Buick. To foreshadow the chaotic energy onboard the ship, which is beyond the mother's control, Ben changed things a bit, creating an outlandish taxi driver who careens through town in a purple Buick.

The bumpy, raucous ride foretells the ship's battle with the ocean's swells during a storm.

I loved Ben's creative idea about a magical orange tree growing onboard the ship. The tree, though, didn't have an important role, except to supply unlimited oranges. Ben did a terrific job expanding the narrative to make the tree a significant part of the story, both as a metaphor and as a foreshadowing element.

Now in Ben's revised version, he explains what happened to the Pickle-Bird Boy. Previously, too much was left untold. Little hints are sprinkled about in a foreshadowing way.

See how many other elements of foreshadowing you can spot in Ben's sea-faring tale. Enjoy the story and have fun.

Loraine McCormick

Loraine McCormick teaches creative writing through the Society of Young Inklings, and she edits children's books. She is a member of the Society of Children's Book Writers and Illustrators. She has a BA in Advertising, with a concentration in English, from San Jose State University. She's worked as a copywriter and as a technical editor. Currently, she is writing several children's picture books, as well as a middle-grade novel. She's raised two sons and lives in San Jose, California, with her husband and a golden doodle named Ginger.

Benjamin Hayes

Benjamin is eleven years old. He likes creating superheroes that fight in Nonth (where Westerndon is located). He also likes to play with his best friends (who are triplets), climb trees, and goof around with his cousin Jack. Jack and Benjamin like to create superheroes together. When he grows up, he wants to be an ornithologist, which is a scientist who studies birds.

Loraine McCormick: What gave you the idea for writing _Whale Watching Past Westerndon_?

> **Benjamin Hayes:** My teacher wanted us to do a writing prompt about a boy or girl who sees a whale for the first time. I was already writing stories about Burt and the Pickle-Bird Man. So this story is actually a prologue to the stories I've already written.

Q: When did you start writing stories?

> **A:** When I was in first grade, I started writing stories about me going to the North Pole and visiting Santa. In fifth grade, I started writing longer stories.

Q: Where do you get your ideas?

> **A:** I like pickles. A lot. I wanted to write a story about a guy who really liked pickles and really liked birds. My cousin and I

always write stories about superheroes and other stuff–World War II and medieval timeframe.

Q: Are you working on a new story?

A: Currently, I have about eight or nine stories going. One is about a boy who turns into a rat. Another is *The Kingdom of Fyrllan*, which is Welsh for flame fire.

Q: Our revision focus was foreshadowing. What changed in the story when you revised or added in foreshadowing elements?

A: It made the story a lot more interesting, and it was fun to try to fit in little bits of information that didn't seem significant at first, but then became very significant at the end of the story.

Q: Do you like your story now that it has been revised?

A: Yes, it's much better. The flow is much better, and it makes a lot more sense.

Q: What advice would you give other writers about revision?

A: Don't be frustrated to make revisions just because you think your old story is good the way it is. Revisions are good. To be honest, I was a little frustrated in the beginning when we first started revising, but now the story is a lot better than it was.

Q: What did you like about the revision process?

A: I learned a lot more about foreshadowing, and that's going to really help me with future stories.

Whale Watching Past Westerndon

from the Nonthian Tales of Olde!

by

Benjamin Hayes

Prologue

On a snowy winter's evening, when the trees were bare and covered with frost, Burt and his good friend the Pickle-Bird Man sat beside the fire in the Pickle-Bird Man's house to rest their old legs and to tell stories. The Pickle-Bird Man had already told numerous tales, and he asked Burt to recount a story from his childhood. Burt smiled, leaned back in his chair, and began his tale….

One blustery fall day, when the wind bit at the noses of townspeople and frost coated the orange trees, a chubby little boy named Burt looked out the window of his room in the village where he lived—a town called Westerndon.

"Mummy!" he cried happily, bouncing for joy. "Is today the day we get to see the Pickle Whales?"

A plump woman with curly brown hair burst into the room.

"Yes, it is, Burt! Aren't you excited? I'm bringing lots of Snickers bars! The boat loads in an hour. We'd better get down to the docks."

Burt grinned and put on a sweater. He was as happy as a mouse in a house built with crumbs and cheese!

A few minutes later, the little boy was out in his front yard with his mother. She hailed a purple Buick that was driving at top speed down the road. It screeched to a halt by their house, and a large macaroni penguin sauntered out. He wore a bowler hat, and clenched in his beak was a long pipe, from which he blew bubbles of all shapes and sizes.

"Hello, there," he drawled lazily. "I'm Gumuloningus, your taxi driver. Hop on in." He ushered them into his brightly colored car.

Gumuloningus plopped into the front seat of the purple Buick and sped off. Burt's mother, who barely had time to buckle her seatbelt, held onto her son for dear life.

Burt, however, was enjoying the ride.

After driving at 120 miles per hour for more than thirty minutes, the penguin finally stopped his car. Burt's mother tottered out of the car, using her son's shoulders for support.

"Never...again," she managed to mumble as she and her son walked toward the docks.

Ships of all sizes and contents lined the dock: ships full of fish; golden ships bearing the Nonthian coat of arms; and small, wind-battered ships made of wood, to name a few. Burt's mother pointed feebly toward a large steamer with the words "Nonthian Whale Watching" emblazoned across the sails in large letters.

They walked toward the steamer, where a young falcon named Bagelore stood to shred their tickets with his beak.

"Come to see the Pickle Whale, I presume?" he said in a voice that was gruff but not unkind–similar to how a walrus might speak.

"Yes, dear," Burt's mother said. "Would you like a Snickers bar?"

"No, thanks," Bagelore said.

"All right," Burt's mother said. "Time to get on the ship!"

Burt stepped up onto the deck, where huge golden pipes fastened to the ship huffed and sputtered smoke. Battered lifeboats leaned against the deck of the ship. An old man crept out of a cabin from the middle of the ship. He was the captain!

"Everybody on?" he asked.

"Yes, sir, I do believe we're the only ones," said Burt's mother.

Suddenly, a crowd of animals and people boarded the ship. Cormorants, seals, and seagulls were intermingling with old men. They all wore matching uniforms.

"Hello!" they all said in unison. "We're the Navy Seals!"

The captain and Burt stifled their laughs. Then the old captain gingerly walked to the front of the ship and shouted "We're off! Bagelore, cut the ropes!"

With his sharp beak, the young falcon snapped the strained ropes that held the ship to the dock, and the boat was swept onto the waves.

For the first hour, Burt looked over the side at all the fish streaming by. There were bronze sharks and crimson octopuses, red roosterfish, and vivid-colored sea slugs. But there was no Pickle Whale in sight, and Burt was growing tired of waiting.

Burt's mother took out her camera and tried to get the captain to pose for one of the many group pictures she was taking, much to the captain's dismay.

Burt lingered by the captain but then decided to climb to the crow's nest to talk to Bagelore, as the captain was mostly silent. Burt was chased down, however, by a family of crows that squawked angrily at him. A ruffled Burt climbed back down the ladder and then sat next to the captain again.

Finally, Bagelore soared down from the crow's nest and stopped the ship. "The Pickle Whale should be surfacing here in about a half hour. It's a good idea to wait here so he can get used to us."

Burt sighed and walked over to a tree on the ship that was bearing many juicy mandarin oranges. This tree, unlike the orange trees in Westerndon, wasn't coated in frost.

"Are these real?" he asked.

The captain grunted a yes and shoved one of the oranges into his mouth.

The plump boy plucked an orange from the tree and, without stopping to peel it, sank in his teeth. Oh, but it was filled with the most marvelous juices! They were simply divine! Burt pocketed a few for later and continued eating the rest of the oranges on the tree. He munched and munched and munched, devouring orange after orange until they were all gone. Burt looked at the tree, which was bare of all fruit.

"Sorry, sir," he said to the captain.

The captain looked up, not noticing the darkening sky. "Well, if my name isn't Caali Calivert, you've eaten all the oranges! Don't worry; they'll grow back in about three minutes. They're Nonthian oranges. My brother and I bought the tree when I was very young. The oranges give you immortality!" Suddenly, the captain's voice grew serious. "But as with some blessings, this blessing also comes with a curse. Any child who eats these oranges will become immortal. But, if a tragedy occurs and that child is separated from his family, he will never be able to return unless the same tragedy happens to another child. Then, the curse will be broken."

"There was once a green-garbed boy who ate oranges off this tree," the captain continued. "He was the son of my brother. He didn't have a name for a while since my brother and his wife just couldn't think of one. One day, the child saw pictures of pickles and waxwing birds, and he loved them, so his parents named him the Pickle-Bird Boy." Caali paused. "Kind of a weird way to get a name. I would have named him Rodulphos or Maximillianus instead."

"Anyway, one day he was on this ship with his mother during a storm. He was supposed to stay in his cabin, but he snuck out at night, and no one ever saw him again. My poor brother! I should have been more careful." The captain dried his teary eyes with the collar of his shirt. "So please be careful."

"On a more cheerful note," the old man finished, "As long as you don't fall off the boat, you'll be fine! Come, let's eat some more oranges and…"

But the man never finished his statement, for Bagelore flew down to the cabin shrieking "Caali! There's a storm brewin'! We've got to go back!"

"Get everyone below the deck!" Caali thundered, pushing past Burt, who was looking over the edge of the boat. "We won't be able to escape this one!"

Before Burt was rushed inside by his mother, he saw a splash of green deep under the water…

Below deck, Burt's mother hugged Burt goodnight and gave him a Snickers bar. She soon drifted off into a dreamless sleep.

Burt, however, couldn't fall asleep. Perhaps it was because of the sugar in the Snickers bar. Perhaps it was because of the snoring of Caali and the Navy Seals. But it was most likely the flash of green Burt had seen in the water.

"It has to be the Pickle Whale," Burt whispered. "It just has to be."

Burt slowly climbed out of his bed and tiptoed past the passengers' cabins and the captain's quarters.

He quietly crept up out of the bottom of the boat and emerged on the top deck, where a wild thunderstorm was clashing with the water and the whale-watching ship. Burt looked up to the crow's nest, where Bagelore and a sodden family of crows were waiting out the storm. They, too, were asleep.

Without warning, a gust of wind knocked into Burt, sending him sprawling. He attempted to get a foothold on the rocking deck of the ship.

In the sea, there was again a brilliant flash of green. A huge fish-like creature was also waiting out the storm...

On the deck, Burt was sliding around like crazy. He tried to clamber back to his cabin, but it was no use. The wind swirled around him angrily, biting at his ears. He slid down the deck until his feet were dangling over the sea. Clinging to the railing, he heaved himself upward, but the wind pushed him down again. He tried to get a better hold on the edge of the boat, but he was no match for the screaming wind and the reaching waves. Giving up, he loosened his aching arms and fell into the sea.

Burt surfaced in the churning water, sputtering and choking. He grabbed hold of a clump of seaweed, which was then torn from his grasp. The little boy couldn't tread water much longer. He swam for a large rock ledge where a flock of pelicans was perched.

He clung to the battered rock, gasping for air. Trying to get away from the waves, he slowly climbed the slippery outcropping. Burt held onto to whatever hold the cliff offered. He grasped mussels and pieces of old seaweed, clams, and even angry yellow crabs. Slowly but surely, he neared the top.

Burt made it to the top of the huge rock, but he was scraped and scratched all over. He was tired and felt helpless, but he had to get back to the ship. The question was how was he ever going to return?

The ship had dropped anchor about three hundred yards away. At least, that's what it seemed like. The fog, clouds, waves, and torrents of rain made it almost impossible to tell.

He sat there, wet and miserable, with his eyes closed, trying to get some rest. After about five minutes, a brownish-colored pelican hopped up to him and gave him a quizzical look. Burt opened his eyes and glared at the creature.

"Go away, bird," he said. "Can't you see I've got no fish?"

The bird narrowed his eyes and moved closer toward Burt. The pelican stared intently at Burt's pocket, where an extra orange from Caali's orange tree resided. The bird plucked it out and waddled over to the edge of the rock.

"Hey!" Burt shouted, getting up to chase the pelican. "Gimme that back!" He sprinted toward the bird, which was hovering over the water. Burt hesitated, then jumped at the bird.

Burt's hand grabbed the orange, but he fell over the ledge. Shouting, he tried to grab the cliff face, but his hands were too far away. He closed his eyes, not seeing the orange, which was glowing and emitting enticing scents. The flash of green reappeared in the water.

At that moment, the rain stopped. Burt sailed downward, preparing to meet his doom. He would hit the water so hard that it would probably kill him.

He saw a sparkle of green in the water. With a huge splash, a green whale surfaced. It was the Pickle Whale! Burt hit the soft folds of the whale's billowy blubber and fainted.

On board the ship, Burt's mother woke up and realized her little son was gone. She cried out in terror and jumped out of her bed, waking up the other passengers. The Navy Seals leaped up, waddled toward her, and gave her some Snickers bars out of her handbag to calm her nerves. They practically had to force-feed her, as she was trying to scramble away from their grasp and search the ship for her lost son.

Caali hobbled over to her and patted her back. "It's okay," he consoled, giving her another Snickers bar. "Chocolate made in Nonth will calm you down. You need to eat some. We'll search the ship for you."

Burt's mother accepted the Snickers bar, but she refused to sit in the cabin and wait for her son. She rushed out of the cabin with the rest of the men.

Captain Caali shuffled out onto the wet deck, looking for Burt. He saw a small boy floating in the water close to the ship. Recognizing Burt, he grabbed a net on the side of the ship and tried to pull the boy in, but Burt was too far away from the ship. The Navy Seals jumped into the water, lifted him out of the waves, and placed him on the deck.

A pelican flew over to the ship and performed CPR on Burt. The boy choked and water streamed out of his open mouth. He sat up and looked around. The pelican seemed to grin. It unfolded its wings and flew off across the water.

"Aye! Thar she is! The Pickle Whale! I can't believe my old eyes and ears! Finally!" Caali cried, overjoyed with excitement.

"Burtie boy!" Burt's mother cried tears of joy as she sprinted toward him, Snickers bars wrappers flying behind her. She held her shivering son in a tight embrace.

Bagelore flew down from the crow's nest, where he had been waiting out the storm. "Hate to interrupt, humans, but what is that?"

"What do you think, Bagelore?" the captain said sarcastically. "Pretty sure it's a whale."

"No," Bagelore said, rolling his eyes. "That thing in the whale's mouth."

Sure enough, there was something or someone wedged in the whale's jaws. Bagelore looked closer—it looked like a human!

Calling to the pelicans and the Navy Seals, he flew into the whale's mouth and lifted the boy out, with the help of the other birds. They lowered the boy onto the deck, who, not unlike Burt, was also a bit round around the waistline. Clutched in his hand were two things: a pickle and a picture of a waxwing bird.

"Who are you?" Caali asked the boy.

"Ahem, Caali, he can't talk!" said Bagelore exasperatedly.

The little boy sat up; he was dressed in drenched green

clothes. "I'm the Pickle-Bird Boy," he answered. "And you must be Uncle Caali."

"My nephew!" Caali cried, running toward him.

The ship's orange tree began to shake, and Caali Calivert started to change. With each step he took, he could run easier. He grew a little taller, and the worry lines on his forehead were gone completely. In fact, he looked as if he had just lost more than twenty years of age. He hugged his nephew for a long, long time.

Once all of the passengers were seated (the Pickle-Whale was floating beside the boat), Caali asked his nephew why he hadn't been able to get back on the boat.

"It's just like you told me so long ago, Uncle Caali," the Pickle-Bird Boy said. "There's a price for the orange's gift of immortality. But now that Burt experienced the same tragedy that I experienced, the curse is broken."

"Oh, and the Pickle Whale's been sheltering me for a long time. I owe him a lot." The green-garbed boy grinned at the huge narwhal-like creature.

The Pickle-Whale blew happily through his blowhole and swam away into the waves.

The boat returned to the harbor in the space of an hour. After saying goodbye to Caali, Bagelore, and the Pickle-Bird Boy (who was staying with his uncle for an undetermined amount of time), Burt and his mother disembarked.

The purple Buick was waiting for them by the side of the boat. Gumuloningus stepped out and tried to usher in Burt and his mother, but Burt's mother pushed him aside.

"We've had enough excitement for one day," she said firmly. "Please call us another taxi."

Gumuloningus looked disappointed, but he consented and got back in his car so he could call another taxi.

Soon, the taxi arrived, driven by a tortoise, and Burt and his mother got in. The car seemed to have picked up some habits from its owner, as it took two hours to get to Westerndon.

After getting out of the taxi and saying goodbye to the tortoise, Burt and his mother walked home for pickles and tea!

Epilogue

"I remember that," said the Pickle-Bird Man. "It was the day I went to live in Westerndon. By the way, whatever happened to that pelican?

"He flew away, and I never saw him again," said Burt sadly.

"Is that so?" mused the Pickle-Bird Man, pointing to the window. "I wonder if that bird up there is him?"

Burt looked out the window, too. A huge brown bird with a large beak was flapping down through the sky. Burt rushed outside to meet the pelican. He landed with a thump on Burt's shoulder.

A slow grin spread across Burt's face. Despite the coldness of the day, he felt warm and cheerful inside. The plump, balding man said a goodbye to the Pickle-Bird Man and ran back to his house to have lunch with his old feathery friend.

Concrete Details

Dear Reader,

Xiomara wrote an eloquent and passionate creative essay that explores deep sorrow, forgiveness, and redemption. While not exactly a fictional story, the narrator goes through an arc of pain, change, and growth. And while it may be based loosely on something the author has experienced personally, she wanted to write about these kinds of emotions in a general and universal way.

At our first revision meeting, we decided that adding more concrete details to the piece and developing the arc of emotion that the anonymous narrator experiences were our goals.

Xiomara wrote an additional 250 words—a full page—and added them throughout her story to flesh-out the emotional arc of the narrator. To help clarify difficult and abstract emotions, she used natural metaphors such as sun and shadow, clouds and birds, water and oceans. She also added sensory details to bring the reader closer to the narrator, such as, "It feels as if you're flying, and the clouds of sweet, almost fluffy moisture brush across your face."

Anytime we can take a concept such as "feeling happy" and make it more concrete, we're strengthening our writing. How can you show that a character feels joy? She might laugh and jump up and down. She can run up and hug her best friend. She can twirl around with her eyes closed and her face turned up to the sun. In your writer's notebook, keep track of gestures you use and things you and others do when you're feeling certain emotions. Then plug them into your stories!

Ann Jacobus

Ann Jacobus has an MFA in Writing for Children and Young Adults from Vermont College of Fine Arts and teaches writers of all ages in the California Bay Area. Her YA thriller, *Romancing the Dark in the City of Light,* was published by St. Martin's Griffin/ Macmillan in 2015.

Xiomara Guevara

Xiomara is twelve years old and attends River Glen Dual Immersion K-8. She loves to draw more than anything and enjoys writing and reading almost as much.

Ann Jacobus: What changed for your story in your revision?

> **Xiomara Guevara:** I tried to clarify certain details, for example, I wrote about the "black box" we crush our emotions into, and I wanted to add that I imagined that it feels like a cage. I also wanted to show how you can transition back into the light from a place of darkness—to sharpen the ending.

Q: How did you come up with your ideas for the changes?

> **A:** I knew I wanted to improve it, so I read it closely. I came up with phrases I wanted to add, and I just had to figure out where to put them. I got my ideas by re-imagining the piece. I always wanted it to be different than a traditional story, one that readers could imagine themselves into and relate to personally.

Q: How do you feel the revisions affected your story?

> **A:** I think my revisions affected the story positively. I got to add things I thought of after I wrote the first draft.

Q: What advice do you have for other young writers who don't like to revise?

A: I don't like to revise, but it helps if you try to imagine what you wish you had put in before. Also, come up with a quote and figure out where to insert it. Add more details. It's really a chance to be creative, like taking a clay model of a dragon and turning it into a three-headed Hydra! You can always delete what you don't like and start over.

Q: What are some of your favorite books?

A: I love Manga and am reading *Kiichi and the Magic Books* by Taka Amano. Another book I really liked was in Spanish, *Hasta el Viento Puede Cambiar de Piel* by Javier Malpica.

Silver Lining

by

Xiomara Guevara

Everybody has a breaking point. That time when you get pushed past your limit, when you want to disappear into oblivion. That time when you wish the ground to swallow you up or to open your eyes from that never-ending nightmare of your life. When moments of joy seem like a distant past or a whole other era. When you feel like crawling into a black hole and flooding the emptiness with oceans of tears.

Everybody feels alone at some point in their lives. At some point, we all believe in our hearts that we don't belong, that we don't fit in. Maybe it was due to betrayal from the person that meant the whole world to us, by a single broken promise that ran blood-deep. Or maybe it was due to hurt to our pride, embarrassment beyond belief. No matter what it was, it was something that shattered our whole world, something powerful enough to drag us into a black hole, never to return.

Emptiness then consumes our hearts, and we do things, unthinkable things, that, in our sane minds, we would never even

imagine doing. When we arrive at this certain point, all we want is to be alone. Alone, anywhere, anyhow. Without a place to go to, we hide. Whether absent in state of mind or in self, we do so.

Some of us crush our deep, dark emotions in a neat little box and throw it to the back of our minds, plastering a smile on top of the pain and suffering we've come to accept as normal. But at one point, the box will overflow with feeling. And that's when the darkness seeps in, takes over, and the tiny box, no matter how sturdy it is, can't hold it all, not anymore. It then opens, giving way to torrents of pain, sorrow, and yearning, all of the need sweeping out in a maelstrom that no one can survive.

And then, when it all comes out, a shadow remains. That shadow is the repentance, the repentance of pushing others away. Of not letting them in to help us in our struggle for internal survival. We wish we'd learned to trust them, but now it's too late.

We stand as the second wave, the wave of realization, of repentance, sweeps upon us. We cry, not because we are weak, but because we refused help from those surrounding us. We let our true, most vulnerable feelings drift along in a sea of tears.

In our misery, we've let others fall into the shadows alongside us, an unforgivable crime. We blame ourselves for everything and fear, most of all, forgiveness. We want it; we want it badly, even to the point of necessity. Yet, we fear it, and we fear it immensely. How could we deserve it? We've done nothing to deserve it. So we run from it, shield ourselves from it in such a cowardly way. We run and hide from it, yet we need and yearn for it just as much. We fear its irrationality but adore its warmth. On the other hand, what we do not realize is that, much like ourselves, these people reaching out need us as much as we need them. They are the same as we are, helping others get away from the darkness that they know so well, while trying to carry the burden of suffering alone. As soon as you realize this—that you are needed—you slowly accept their exit ticket from the dark cave while guiding them out at the same time.

As you exit the shadow and enter the light, you lose every trace of the abyss you came from, except the memory. The memory is what makes you kind. You wish to relieve others from the darkness you experienced for so long. You teach others that the darkest shadow comes from the brightest of lights. That the shadow that follows them makes them kind. After all, without clouds, a sunset isn't as beautiful. That the only way to bring others upward is to be at the top, pulling them up. As you help others, you grow happier and farther from that shadow. You let the world, the beautiful world, surround you. It feels as if you're flying, and the clouds of sweet, almost fluffy, moisture brush across your face. Like when you feel light and breezy, as if in a dream. As if the cosmos, so far away, whisper with mystery into your ear. As you grin and giggle at newfound friends who share sentiments from the past. As the sun sets and your shadows grow long. As the weight of the world lifts off your shoulders into the sky, soaring like a bird. And you smile, a smile from the heart, a smile from the depths of your soul, like you haven't in a long time.

Pacing

Patrick York mentored Judge Cantrell through a revision focused on pacing in Judge's story, *The Ghost of the Underworld*.

Dear Reader,

The Ghost of the Underworld is a suspenseful story about overcoming fear and adversity. After Jake's parents leave on their anniversary vacation, he persuades his friends to wander into a forbidden forest to find a mysterious ghost they've all heard has taken the lives of people silly enough to have ventured deep within the woods. Though at first they don't believe the rumors to be true, they discover a dark secret waiting in the forest that none of them were prepared to find.

Because of the large number of interesting locations and events in the story, Judge and I focused on pacing. We worked on providing the protagonist with moments of personal reflection and expanding descriptions of the story's locations.

Looking into your character's mind is an easy way to give your reader some breathing room. When a story seems to be moving along at a break-neck speed and the intensity has plateaued, a great way to keep your audience connected to your character's perspective is to give them a chance to see how she or he is reacting to the events of the story. The easiest way to achieve this is to ask yourself what you know about the type of person your character is, then reflect on how a person like that would react in a given situation.

Reflecting on how your character would react is most important following moments of disruption in your character's life. Say your character's dog escapes from his backyard, and your character exhausts himself chasing the dog down the street. He helplessly watches his best friend run away. Readers can truly connect to your character's situation on his slow walk back home if you, as the writer, go into his mind and tell us his thoughts. What was it like when his family first brought the dog back from the pound? What will it be like tomorrow when the dog doesn't wake up your character by licking his hand like he always did?

Expanding a description of a location is another great way to slow the pace of a narrative and give your reader the opportunity to immerse themselves in the story rather than letting the events pass without being able to thoroughly imagine the places your character passes through. As your character moves from place to place, without considerable moments of description, it can be easy for your readers to forget where your character is and how this location affects his decisions and the details of his story. Remember to consider sights, sounds, temperatures, the quality of light, the business or lack thereof when your character enters a new place. Also, consider how each new place may affect your character. Is it too loud to hear in the cafeteria? Is it too dark to see in the backyard at night? Does the sound of the trees groaning under the wind make your character apprehensive to enter the forbidden forest?

All stories should be exciting in some way, but a well-paced story means giving your readers the opportunity to immerse themselves in the thoughts and locations of your characters.

Patrick Garrett York

Patrick York is from the Mojave Desert of California. He received his MFA from the University of California, Riverside, where he was a Gluck Fellow of the Arts. He lives in Los Gatos, California, with his wife.

Judge Cantrell

Judge just finished sixth grade at Eastside Prep. He was born in San Francisco but spent most of his childhood living in Nevada. He likes writing, reading, and acting. He and his friend Corey are currently working on a movie script about superheroes.

Patrick York: First, how did the revision go?

> **Judge Cantrell:** I think the revision went well. I followed your advice to the bone, and I deeply thought about what my character might be feeling. So I added dialogue and thoughts so the reader wouldn't be left behind.

Q: Do you think it was difficult? Easy? Did it turn out well? Could it have turned out better?

> **A:** At some points, it was difficult, time-wise–trying to take care of everything on time–but at some points, it was really easy because thoughts were flying off the top of my head.
> It was a good 60/40. I enjoyed 60 percent, and 40 percent was difficult. I just wanted to have fun with it, and I didn't feel like it was an assignment for school. And I felt like there was always room for improvement like with anything: sports, school. So I just tried to have fun with it.

Q: Let's talk about what you did. How did you start?

A: I first thought about the notes I took during our first meeting, starting at the part where the characters enter the forest. I thought about what I would do in my main character's shoes, and I asked myself the questions he would ask himself. I put myself in the shoes of an eleven-year-old kid and imagined what he was thinking. Is the forest a trap? What do I do here in a place where the branches could reach out and grab me at any second?

Q: When you were writing it, did you read it out loud?

A: Sometimes, yes. Sometimes, like when I got more in-depth and had a great idea that I had to get on paper, I wrote more than I read it out loud. In revising, it was about 70 percent reading out loud and looking for places where a new idea might fit in.

Q: Did you ever read your story out loud to an audience? Did they applaud you afterward?

A: I read it out loud to my sixth-grade class, and they were really appreciative and supportive of my story and my effort. Yeah, they applauded me when they found out that I'd got in. My friend Corey submitted a poem, but it wasn't accepted, but the class applauded him for his efforts, and that's what I like about Corey: he goes for it even if he's not accepted because that's what's really important. I have a little sister whose birthday is in two days, but I haven't read it out loud to her or my parents either.

Q: Do you like to read? Are you a reader?

A: My more in-depth reading started with *Geronimo Stilton*, but then I started reading books like *Diary of a Wimpy Kid*. I like reading for the same reason that I like acting. I like to think of myself acting out scenes from the stories as an actor on the big screen. I'm reading the *Platypus Police Squad* about platypus detectives in a police squad. The city is run by a panda, but his head of security doesn't trust him. The head of security's gotta protect the panda but also protect the city. I'm waiting for it to come out on the Book Mobile, which is a moving truck of books and movies. My family and I go down and check out books and movies for two weeks, and then we return them. The next book in the *Platypus* series is out now, and I hope I see it at the Book Mobile the next time it comes around.

Q: Did you grow up around here?

A: I was born in San Francisco and raised in Nevada. My sister is the opposite. Sometimes I do miss Vegas, but I do not miss the weather. My father used to work at the Mini Grand Prix, and one time, we got to celebrate my fourth birthday there.

Q: Are you working on any other projects?

A: Khan Academy: all sorts of things involving math. The other thing is not really a project because it's not going to go global, but I'm working with Corey on a movie right now regarding superheroes. We make up our own superheroes. My character is the Dream. Whatever he dreams about, he becomes. Another is a master of the bow and arrow and has a black belt. Corey's character is Dan. It's like a civil war type movie. We're still looking for a crew and a camera to shoot it.

The Ghost
of the Underworld

by

Judge Cantrell

Chapter One

All right, so this story is not what you think it is. It might get creepy along the way, so I suggest that you stop reacing halfway through.

My name is Jake, and I have been tc the underworld. Why, you might wonder? Well, it all started with my parents and their anniversary cruise. They went on and on abou: what I could and could not do.

"Make sure you take your vitamins arid eat your vegetables. Don't stay up too late, and under no circumstances should you go into the forest."

"Wait, why can't I go into the forest?" I asked.

At that moment, my mom, Susan, was calling one of her friends who's like seventy (well, not really, but you get the gist) to watch me for the week. My dad, John, was getting their passports. So to be honest, my question about the forest never got answered until mom's friend Mike told this story:

"Legend has it that a group of adults went into that forest two blocks down and got their souls taken by the ghost of the underworld."

It happened to be the same forest my parents were talking about.

"Were the bodies ever found?" I asked.

"No, they haven't found the bodies yet, and I personally don't think they will," Mike said.

That's when I knew it. That's when I realized that I was gonna be the one to stop that ghost and bring him to justice, but not alone, of course. No, I was gonna need some help, and I knew just the right people.

Chapter Two

"No way man, oh, heck to the no. Are you out of your big-headed mind?"

"Randy's got a point, Jake. It is too dangerous to go out there into that forest."

These were the responses of my best friends, Randy and Stella. We would do everything together. One time, we were in this talent show, and we tried to do magic, but that did not work out so well. Randy accidently spilled some of the milk that we were using for this trick where you pour milk into paper, and it just disappears. Yeah, well, he must have done something very wrong because he went to show the audience that the milk was gone, and milk poured out onto Stella's head. Those two have always been there for me, but this time around, it was a different story.

"Come on, guys, level with me here. I mean, how awesome would it be if three middle schoolers from Eastside College Prep could pull off the bust of the century and be heroes? Tell me, does that not sound cool to you guys?" I was really hoping that this would be the game changer.

"Fine, but if I lose a leg, it's all on you man, you got me," Randy said.

"Yeah, me too. Unlike this guy, I'm dead serious," Stella added.

That's when I knew this was gonna be a journey to remember.

"So let's cover some ground rules while we are at it," I said. "First, we always stick together no matter what happens. Second, we do not wander off alone, especially at night."

"Let me make one," Randy said impatiently. "Next, we always try to help each other out no matter what."

"Finally, the most important rule of all…," I said.

And, in unison, we said, "NO ONE TELLS THEIR PARENTS!"

After that, we started to go over game plans for out in the forest. This was so exciting; I felt like I was in the movie *Percy Jackson and the Lightning Thief*. I was Percy trying to clear my name. But I knew I wasn't. I was simply out to put an end to this ghost of the underworld.

Chapter Three

Well, it was the big day–Wednesday. I had just three days to go out there and find that ghost and bring him to justice.

"You guys ready for the adventure of a lifetime?" I asked.

I was about to say something else when a familiar voice interrupted my thoughts.

"Jake, I'm coming with you," yelled Mike, standing behind us.

"What? You cannot go out there; you'll die!" I said cautiously.

"It's okay; I will be fine. Besides, you're gonna need an adult anyway," he said confidently.

"I can't ask you to do this, Mike; it's just too much," I said. "You cannot go; you have to stay here."

"Oh, come on," Randy said, "Let him go, you know what they say, the older, the wiser."

Then I was convinced. "All right then, what are we waiting for? Let's do it."

And with that, we set out for the best adventure in the history of adventures.

Chapter Four

When I first walked into the forest on Wednesday, I got quite a scare. There were branches that looked like they would reach out and grab you, and trees that looked like they were gonna fall over on top of you any minute. Was I scared? Yes, but I was still determined to stop this ghost, and I was not turning back now.

"Is it just me or is this place creepy?" Stella asked.

"Yep, definitely creepy," I said.

"WATCH OUT, JAKE!" Mike yelled.

I turned around, and, like I said, a tree was falling right to the ground. So as fast as I could, I moved out of the way of the tree, but one of the branches clipped my arm.

"Are you all right?" Randy asked.

"Yeah, a little bit," I said.

We looked at the tree in disbelief. *Was that an attack from the ghost?* I asked myself this question over and over and still had no answer. With that, we kept on walking in the dark, treacherous, and malevolent forest.

"This is getting boring. Where is the action? Where is the fun?" Randy said. "I didn't sign up for walking."

"Oh, would you calm down?" Stella said. "Life is not always fun and games, so…"

All of a sudden, we heard a sort of screeching sound and saw a shadowy figure in the distance. As it approached, the forest got darker.

"JAKE, HELP ME! PLEASE!" Mike shouted.

I turned around, and I saw that Mike was hanging upside down by the leg.

"STOP LOOKING FOR ME OR ELSE THEY'RE NEXT!" the ghost said in a raspy voice.

With that, the light was back, and Randy, Stella, and I were still deep in the forest. The ghost was gone, but, more importantly, Mike was gone!

Chapter Five

"I'm going after him," I said. "Don't try to stop me!" It was 4:30 on Thursday afternoon, and we had no adult help or wisdom about this forest. "This is all my fault," I said.

"Don't say that, Jake. It's not your fault." Stella said.

"It is," I said. "If I had said 'no' like I should have, then he would not be gone right now."

"Jake, if you're going, then so am I," Randy said.

"Me, too!" Stella agreed.

"Then what are we waiting for?" I said. "Let's do—"

"BAD CHOICE, JAKE." The ghost raised his hand and suddenly two demon spirits emerged from the ground and started to chase us.

"Run!" I yelled.

And we ran, trying to shake off the spirits that were tailing us.

"GOTCHA!" said the spirits, grabbing my friends.

"No!" I said. And with that, Randy and Stella were gone, leaving me the Lone Ranger.

Chapter Six

That's it! I'm sick of it! No one messes with my friends and gets away with it! Oh heck to the no. I was going to find this ghost, but how? I just remembered that old Mike had left me with a compass to guide us to the lair of the ghost. I hoped that this would really guide me to the cave or lair, or whatever that ghost lives in. The compass led me in every direction that it could. Now I know never to use a compass. Anyway, I was still very determined to find this ghost once and for all. I wasn't stopping anytime soon.

Time passed, and I had finally found it, the ghost's hideout. "Time to get my friends back," I said. "Let's do this."

"Well, what do we have here? Little Jake is here to be the hero," the ghost sang.

"Where are my friends?" I yelled.

"Oh, I'm so glad you asked. Bring them in, boys!" yelled the ghost.

"Guys!" I yelled.

"JAKE. HELP!" they all screamed.

"SILENCE!!!" yelled the ghost. "The only way you shall ever be free is if your friend Jake here gives himself as a sacrifice and is taken to the underworld with me for the rest of eternity."

"WHAT?" they all screamed.

"Do we have a deal, Jake, or will it be the last you see of your friends?" asked the ghost.

"Okay, I'll do it. I'll go with you to the underworld."

"What?" exclaimed Stella.

"No!" yelled Randy.

"You don't have to do this. Besides, what will your parents say if I don't have you home tomorrow?" said Mike.

"Guys, don't worry. The only reason I'm here is to save you. That's all. And if this is what it takes, then so be it. And you know what? Maybe the underworld is not so bad."

"Oh, it's bad, all right. Badder than anything you've ever seen," said the ghost. Enough chit-chat. It's time to say goodbye to your friends and hello to your new life."

"Bye guys, it's been really great knowing you. Promise me you'll always KEEP IT TIGHT!" With that, I left planet Earth for the final time, or so people thought.

Chapter Seven

In the underworld, things are different, way different. The temperature is really hot, but the ghost said that I would get used to it. I guess the ghost really wanted me secure because he put a lot of guards around my cell. I tried some small talk with them, but they would not have it.

Time went by that day, and I thought I would never get out. Restless, I paced around my cell. To my surprise, I found a hidden letter. It read:

> *Jake,*
>
> *We have been watching you, and we are very impressed with what you have accomplished over this past week even though it was strictly against your parents' rules that you shall not go into the forest. You showed that you were very determined to get that ghost and take him down. For your bravery, courage, and determination, we hereby give you this power source to free yourself from the underworld. But you must first complete three tasks. First, get out of the cell and pass the guards. Next, climb up the oil-covered rock wall. Be careful because it's slippery. Finally, get past the ghost, and the power source is all yours.*
>
> *Sincerely,*
> *The Guardians of the Sky.*

Wow, I have the opportunity to get out, but I must first complete the ultimate test. Step one: Take out the guards. I wasn't exactly sure how to do this, but I thought I might have an idea.

"Hey, mister guards. Come, I wanna show you a magic trick." I said. To my surprise, it worked. As they came closer, I grabbed their hands and pulled inward. Both of their faces hit the metal bars of my cell. The key to my cell was in a guard's pocket. I grabbed the key, unlocked my cell, and then locked the guards in my cell. I was free. One task down, two to go.

Chapter Eight

My next task was to climb up the oil-covered rock wall. No biggie, I thought, but I thought wrong. Every attempt was useless thanks to the oil on the wall. I kept trying and trying and trying until an idea popped into my head. It was genius. I ripped off the sleeves of my jacket, tied them on my arms like gloves, and, it turns out, it actually worked. I got up the wall on my first try with the sleeves. Two tasks down, one to go. But I knew that the task was no ordinary day at the park.

"Hey, Ghost, where you at? I need to talk with you," I yelled.

"How did you get out of your cell?" he screamed.

"Little something called the Guardians of the Sky."

"NO! I have always hated those pests," he said in a dreadful way.

With that, I tried to run past the ghost. But with an exhale of his awful breath, I was blown back. After a good ten attempts at this, I had to think of something new. Then I realized that the ghost was really tall, so I thought back on two movies where really tall people needed to be brought down–*Captain America: Civil War* and *The Empire Strikes Back.*

"Hey, Ghost, ever seen that really old movie *The Empire Strikes Back*, where they're on the snow planet with the walking things?" I asked.

"What? No. What are you talking about anyway?" he said.

"This," I said as I picked up a grappling hook rope and threw it at his legs. I went round and round and round. I did this as I sang "Ring Around the Roses."

"Ring around the roses, pockets full of posies, ashes, ashes, theghost falls down," I sang. With that, the ghost tumbled back but would not fall. So I decided to throw a rock at him like David and Goliath. I found the biggest rock I could and chucked it. And the ghost came tumbling down.

"The bigger they are, the harder they fall!" I said triumphantly. Just then, I saw the white glowing orb. I knew that was it—the power source. That was my Get-Out-of-Jail-Free card. So as the ghost was coming to, I teased him and said, "Hey, Mister Ghost, see you later, sucka!"

"What? How did you get that?" yelled the ghost.

"It's called raw determination. Sayonara, punk!" I teased.

"NOOOOO!!!" screamed the ghost.

And with that, I was out of there in a heartbeat.

Chapter Nine

"He was like a brother to me, the way he would always help me study. Now I will never get to tell him that," cried Randy.

"Oh, it's okay, Randy. At least we know, and maybe his spirit heard it," Stella said cheerfully.

"Yep, my spirit definitely heard that one," I said, standing behind them.

"Oh, my gosh, you're still here—alive! Thank the God in heaven you're okay!" Mike exclaimed.

After that, I told them how I found a power source that was given to me by the Guardians of the Sky. After we reunited, I figured it was probably best if we got back to my home before my parents did. It was already 1:00 a.m., and my parents would return at 3:00 a.m.; we had only two hours to get back home and act like nothing ever happened. Without hesitation, we ran as fast as we could, making sure not to leave anyone behind.

Chapter Ten

It took a while, but we were finally back where we had started in the forest. We decided we had time to kill and that we could walk back to my house.

"Hey, you guys! Wanna stay at my place for the night and go home later in the day?" I asked Stella and Randy.

They both shrugged and said, "Sure!"

It was 2:45 a.m. when we got back to my house, and we had some cleaning to do before we could rest. Besides, we needed to clean for the homecoming of my parents. We picked up dirty clothes and washed dishes. Stella and Randy helped me clean my room while Mike cleaned his room. When we were finished, there was nothing left to do, and it was already 3:00 a.m. I got out the sleeping bags as fast as I could for Stella, Randy, and me. We lay there, looking up at the ceiling, thinking about different things. Suddenly, the door popped open, and my parents walked in.

"Hey, guys," I said, trying to sound tired, "Mike said I could have some friends over for a sleepover."

"That is fine, sweetheart, go back to sleep," my mom said. "But tell me something first, did you have fun?" she asked.

"Oh, you bet!" I said.

With that, I closed my eyes, thinking of what my next journey would be.

Dedicated to:
My family and the entire Eastside College Prep Family; and, of course, God.

Word Choice

Jena Brigantino mentored Jasper Micheletti through a revision focused on word choice in Jasper's poem, "Beautiful Long Curly Hair."

Dear Reader,

"Beautiful Long Curly Hair" is a lovely poem about the author's little brother. In a poem, there are very few words, and it is clear that Jasper chose each one carefully. He chose active verbs and concrete nouns. Jasper also chose comparisons that allow the readers to pause and enjoy the "mind picture" the words form.

In his revision process, Jasper worked on word choice and how it affects the tone of the poem. We discovered that the lines that stood out the most were the lines with fewer words. Jasper read the poem out loud multiple times and ended up shortening a few lines and finessing his word choice. Jasper's dedication to his work is inspiring. I hope you enjoy "Beautiful Long Curly Hair" by Jasper Micheletti.

Jena Brigantino

Jena Brigantino grew up playing outdoors in California where she dreamed up stories featuring animals. She wishes she could have participated in an Inklings program as a child. As Managing Director of SYI, she strives to extend the opportunity to as many children as possible. Jena holds a BA in Creative Arts with a minor in Education from San Jose State University. In her spare time, Jena enjoys spending time with her big Italian family where memorable stories are constantly shared...loudly!

Jasper Micheletti

Jasper is a second grader who really likes soccer. Jasper loves treating everyone with kindness and wishes the world were less violent. But he still enjoys a good imaginary battle every now and then. Jasper really loves his family.

Jena Brigantino: When did you start writing?

> **Jasper Micheletti:** I've been a writer since I was in kindergarten. I really started writing poems and stories in first grade in Mrs. Grant's class.

Q: How did you come up with the idea for your poem?

> **A:** My brother wrote a poem about me, so I wanted to write one about him.

Q: How do you feel about the revisions you made in "Beautiful Long Curly Hair?"

> **A:** I feel confident, and I'm happy with the changes in sentence length.

Q: What advice do you have for other Inklings who don't like revision very much?

> **A:** I recommend reading your poem or story out loud to a lot of different people. I would tell them to "be confident in yourself" and ask a grown-up to help you.

Beautiful Long Curly Hair

by

Jasper Micheletti

My brother's hair shimmers in the sun.
It is beautiful when he has it up in a bun.
But it is sad when I see him crying when he gets it brushed.

He is crazy.
Once he almost broke my finger when he swung his sword so hard.
He is a little brother, but he is still good with a sword.
He is a barbarian, his hair floating through the air.
He is a samurai, his hair as still as a statue.
He trains almost every day.

His hair looks like a colony of angry bees swarming at his enemies.
His hair looks like a raging wave splashing on his foes.
In battle, he is like an uncontrolled herd of buffalos trampling all the
trees in the forest.

Aram the great.
The warrior.
My little brother.

Humorous Exaggeration

Naomi Kinsman mentored Juliana Baltz through a revision focused on humor through exaggeration in Juliana's poem, "Whale-Eating Contest."

Dear Reader,

Juliana Baltz dove in and allowed herself to be completely wacky with her poem, "Whale-Eating Contest." I'm positive that her favorite poet, Shel Silverstein, would be proud of how the poem turned out. Her spot-on word choice, the characters' extraordinary names, and the delightful rhythm and rhyme all make this poem a complete joy to read out loud.

As we began our revision, the strong rhyme was also one of our biggest challenges. If we started adding to or changing the poem, would the sound of the poem be thrown off? Juliana wanted to change the end of the poem but wasn't sure how to go about the process. At first, we thought maybe a small change would be best. However, as Juliana started thinking about it, she realized she could make the poem even more funny by using the strategy of exaggeration. She remembered how Shel Silverstein sometimes lists all the terrible things that might happen in his poems. Juliana thought it would be fun to experiment with a list of her own.

The second stanza used to read:

It's over, we should give her perk for being a jerk.
Oh that wouldn't work.
You know what?
Let's give her the prize. But that wouldn't be wise.
Oh well goodbye.

You'll see in a few pages how Juliana expanded these lines and made the new section just as amusing as the rest of her poem. Her revision took a lot of courage and perseverance. At first, some of the lines simply refused to rhyme. However, Juliana isn't one to easily give up. In the end, the new section turned out to be her favorite part of the poem.

I was inspired by Juliana's approach to her revision. She dared to stretch and challenge herself. Instead of deciding that what she had was good enough—she had won a writing contest with her original poem, after all—she stuck with the process and made her poem even better than it already was.

If you'd like to play with writing and revising funny poetry, notice Juliana's approach. First, she started with an idea that made her laugh. Next, she played with silly words, unusual names, and outrageous situations. Once she had her draft, she read through for any parts that didn't feel finished. Then, she used the strategy of exaggeration to fill those sections with humor. Juliana also read her poem out loud to others. Her listeners gave her feedback to help her decide how to make the poem as funny as it could be. And I'm telling you…this poem is hilarious. Go on, go read it for yourself!

Naomi Kinsman

Naomi Kinsman is the author of the *From Sadie's Sketchbook* series and the award-winning *Spilled Ink, a Writer's Commonplace Book*. Most recently, Naomi co-authored the *Glimmer Girls* series with recording artist, Natalie Grant. Through a decade of writing and directing plays for young people, and serving as a resident artist in classrooms across the country, Naomi developed Writerly Play, which uses game-based strategies and tools to teach young writers. Naomi also founded Society of Young Inklings. She holds a BA in Theatre Arts from Seattle Pacific University and an MA in Writing for Children and Young Adults from Hamline University.

Juliana Baltz

Juliana is in third grade at Stevenson PACT Elementary School in Mountain View. She enjoys coding JavaScript, biking on Shoreline Hill, playing with friends, and drawing. Juliana loves animals, especially her two pet rats, Cody and Spencer. Her favorite books are *The Babysitters Club* graphic novels and the *Harry Potter* series.

Naomi Kinsman: Do you know where the idea for this poem began?

Juliana Baltz: Shel Silverstein wrote a poem about a girl eating a whale in 60 years, and I thought it was really funny. I wanted to write a poem that was similar about a girl eating a whale.

Q: How would you describe our revision process?

A: We started with one line, and we added some ideas. We had to revise the old lines to work with the new ideas, and, over time, the old parts and the new ideas came together. I added lines to make the poem more rhythmic. The end chunk was a bit short, so I added the "what if" lines. In my original poem, I thought the question of whether we should give Big Molly Bulp the prize was unresolved.

Q: Were you concerned about messing up your poem when we started playing with the end lines?

A: Maybe. I wasn't sure how to resolve the question because

I didn't know how to rhyme the new lines. I wasn't sure if I should give her the prize because I think it could be funny either way. In real life, if you won, you'd get the prize. I wanted to know what would be most funny to other people.

Q: Did you learn anything new in the revision process?

A: If you mention an idea, it's important to come back to that idea later on and resolve it.

Q: Do you have advice for other young people who are writing poetry?

A: If you're unsure of what to do, I think of all the rhymes to a word, like "mouse, house, louse," and I pick the one that would be the funniest. I also think about which word would work best. If you're trying to be funny, you can also make up a word. I think that funny poems are the best kinds of poems.

Q: Do you have a favorite line in the poem?

A: I like the "what if" section best. That's the part we added in the revision. I particularly liked how it turned out.

Whale Eating Contest

by

Juliana Baltz

Whale-eating contest! Whale-eating contest!
The prize is rather big,
a trumpet, a lamp, a bed that's damp,
and a magical singing twig.
A goose, a moose, some fleece, and a niece.
Some bread that's stale, a cuckoo quail.
And a stylish necklace for your calf,
and that is just about half.
Little Lily Stout dropped right out.
But, Big Molly Bulp ate it all in one gulp,
while Petty Petunia Laright was still on her very first bite.
Molly's mother said, "We should give her tons of toys."
Molly's father just sighed and said, "Ohh boy."

It's over, we should give her perk for being a jerk.
Oh, that wouldn't work.
What if she and the magical twig
Opened a street show that went berserk?
What if she bagged up the goose and the moose
who got fat as balloons eating moldy couscous?
What if she gave the fleece to the niece
who knitted green slippers that weren't in one piece?
What if she sold the necklace and the cow
And got enough money to fly to Pulau?
You know what?
Let's give her the prize.
Even though it wouldn't be wise.

Wait, wait, one more thing,
Molly sure did have an appetite,
That whale will probably keep her up all night.

Line Breaks

Patricia Pinedo mentored Cianna Brown through a revision focused on line breaks in Cianna's poem, "Races."

Dear Reader,

The following poem is the strongest piece of writing that I have ever seen from such a young person. Cianna's talents are numerous, and I am very proud that I was given the task of mentoring her.

Cianna's poem is a fascinating and deeply reflective piece. I was moved by the imagery and by the small hints of the tragedy that were conveyed. I believed the best way to bring out more of this sorrowful moment would be to work on disrupting the reader through line breaks, which I decided would be our revision focus. Line breaks are the moments when an author ends one sentence of the poem, or anything that the poem has begun, and causing the rhythm to be disjointed.

There are moments in the poem in which the flow seems to be disrupted, which connects to the idea of the disruption that was caused by the explosion. I wanted to explore this more with Cianna as we worked together. I believed that line breaks would help give the poem a more disjointed look as well as help to place emphasis on the horrific act itself. This would also allow the poem's rhythm to make the reader get lost in a sudden confusion.

I am very proud of the work that Cianna did, and I hope, reader, that you will understand the important message that Cianna displays in the poem. It takes great courage to write about such horrific acts. I am sure that we will see more great things in the future from this emerging writer.

Patricia Pinedo

Patricia Pinedo has been writing poetry since junior high when she was published in a school district-wide publication. She graduated from UC Santa Cruz with a BA in Literature with an emphasis in Creative Writing-Poetry. Her poetry has been published in literary journals. She has completed her Masters in Fine Arts in Creative Writing at San Jose State. She has been a substitute teacher for the past fours years and has worked with a wide range of grade levels. Patricia is excited to be working with the Society of Young Inklings in helping young students develop their storytelling skills that will help them grow in their writing.

Cianna Brown

Cianna is a seventh grader who loves to read, write, and cook. She is involved in Girls Inc., where she is learning to be a carefree, creative, and free-spirited young lady. At Girls Inc., she cooks, does yoga, and enjoys dance. Cianna's favorite subjects in school are English and woodshop. Cianna lives in Oakland with her twin sister, mom, maternal grandparents, aunt, uncle, and her brother who is expected in June 2016. Oh, we can't forget her puppy Cinnamon aka Cinnamelt.

Patricia Pinedo: What inspired you to write this poem?

Cianna Brown: I thought back to a book I read in the sixth grade that told about the 16th Street Baptist Church bombings and gave depictions of life in Birmingham in the early 1960s.

Q: How would you describe the revision process?

A: I kept on reading it over and making sure that everything flowed smoothly and that it synced to my passion about the subject.

Q: How did you make the decisions you did to revise?

A: By trusting my instinct.

Q: What were the easiest and most difficult parts of revising this poem?

> **A:** The easiest part was writing it because I remembered the book I was reading, and I just had to think back to it. The hardest part was finding the appropriate words to fit and making sure that it made sense for the reader.

Q: What are your thoughts about revision in general?

> **A:** That I had made a great choice on where to put my edits and that they're in the correct place.

Q: What advice do you have for other young writers who are working on poetry?

> **A:** To follow your heart and write. Even our fragmented thoughts can evolve into literary masterpieces.

Races

by

Cianna Brown

4 girls dancing like flowers

In the fresh air

White dress and black shoes

Filled with excited souls

The coming to death's door

In minutes' time will be here

A moment's shock

A dark entity will come and

Change the world and lives

Will be lost Moms and Dads a sea of tears Dads' and

Moms' hearts ripped out by the Devil's life is hard in Birmingham

When life gets hard in Birmingham

You don't just walk away you fight

For everyone's land and free will do

Decide the fate of working souls but
Evil stole with sorrow surely untold
The lives of innocence and hope and cut the cord, from earthly
deeds evil
Will come and take away innocent souls
Harsh, horrible hatred from white people
The holy house of hope from God didn't save those 4 little girls
But, it did save some people
The innocence and sorrow that people
Had to suffer in Birmingham
Excited souls ready to go and sing in
Church White wicked ways are evil and
Very powerful and hurt black people and
Moms and Dads and suffering souls dealing
With racist comments no more for 4 souls
Help heal the hollow hearts and freedom rings Today

In Memory of Addie, Denise, Cynthia, and Carole

Specific Details

Naomi Kinsman mentored Kendra Mills through a revision focused on word choice in Kendra's poem, "Leaves."

Dear Reader,

Choosing just-right words for a poem can be a challenge. How do you know whether to pick one word over another? Kendra Mills's poem, "Leaves," stood out to our team of readers right away because of her strong word choice. When Kendra and I met to revise her poem, there definitely wasn't anything that needed fixing in the poem. However, we wondered whether the poem might hold possibilities that Kendra hadn't yet explored.

Kendra's poem ended with the lines:

And drop on the ground for somebody
to come and see

We brainstormed about the many people who might walk by and see the leaf on the ground. We thought about what those people might do when they saw the leaf. Kendra came up with many excellent ideas. In the end, Kendra decided to keep her poem simple. She decided not to include specific examples which would have changed the poem and made it much longer. Instead, she chose to change just a few words in the last lines to hint at her expanded ideas. You'll see her final version on the next pages. Kendra also included a few color words in the first lines to describe the leaf because as we brainstormed, she imagined what kind of leaf might best catch a passerby's eye.

Kendra did two very important things that all writers must do while revising. First, she gave herself room to play and brainstorm many more ideas than she might need in her poem. Sometimes, brainstorming isn't easy to do. We want our writing to be perfect, and we only want to come up with the ideas we actually will use in our work. The problem with this approach, however, is that we limit ourselves. Sometimes the idea we most need never pops to mind. When we have more ideas than we need, we can pick and choose. However, picking and choosing can also be difficult.

The second important thing Kendra did was to make choices. Sometimes we worry about wasting the ideas we worked so hard to brainstorm, so we try to stuff everything into our final work. This approach can make our writing cluttered and confusing. I was impressed with the way Kendra identified the ideas that would add to her original poem while keeping its original simplicity.

If you're writing poetry, you might try Kendra's revision approach. Read over your poem, and find lines that could be more specific. Then, brainstorm. List at least five ways you might make those lines into a detailed example of your big-picture idea. Then, look back at your poem. Do your new ideas make you want to change your poem in any way? Make choices about what to include and what to leave out. Remember, like Kendra, you may change only a word or two, but you might find that even a few slight changes will make your poem even more of what you wanted it to be.

Naomi Kinsman

Naomi Kinsman is the author of the *From Sadie's Sketchbook* series and the award-winning *Spilled Ink, a Writer's Commonplace Book*. Most recently, Naomi co-authored the *Glimmer Girls* series with recording artist, Natalie Grant. Through a decade of writing and directing plays for young people, and serving as a resident artist in classrooms across the country, Naomi developed Writerly Play, which uses game-based strategies and tools to teach young writers. Naomi also founded Society of Young Inklings. She holds a BA in Theatre Arts from Seattle Pacific University and an MA in Writing for Children and Young Adults from Hamline University.

Kendra Mills

Kendra is in the first grade at Graystone Elementary. She likes sports and has played basketball and soccer and is on a swim team called the Dolphins. Kendra also likes animals and has a dog named Honey and a cat named Mr. Peabody. She takes horse riding lessons, too. She also enjoys baking and cooking. Kendra loves to write and draw. She can often be found doing tricks with her hula hoops or riding her bike with her brother and sister.

Naomi Kinsman: What do you like about writing?

Kendra Mills: It lets you use your imagination.

Q: Where did you get the idea for this poem?

A: There are lots of trees in my backyard, and I like to rake the leaves into piles so I can jump in them.

Q: In your revision, you played with options to help a reader imagine the person who saw the leaf. Was it easy or hard to come up with ideas?

A: It was easy to come up with ideas during the revisions.

Q: In the end, you changed a few words of your poem after you played with ideas. What do you think of the finished poem now?

A: I like the finished poem better now.

Q: Do you think it's a good idea for writers to play around with their words and ideas when they revise?

> **A:** Yes, I think it is a good idea for writers to play around with words because it can make what you wrote more interesting than it was.

Q: What advice would you give to other young writers who are working on writing poetry?

> **A:** I would tell them to change it if it makes you happy and proud.

Q: What do you like to read?

> **A:** I like to read chapter books.

Q: Do you ever get stuck when you're creating something? If so, do you have any strategies that help you get unstuck?

> **A:** Sometimes I get stuck with things, but I work on something different and come back to it later.

Leaves

by

Kendra Mills

Red and yellow leaves
fall
from a tree
and float in the air
as slow as a snail.
They drop on the
ground
for everyone
to see.

Rhythm in Poetry

Laura Schmidt mentored Rafael Stankiewicz through a revision focused on rhythm in Rafael's poem, "Long Lost Love."

Dear Reader,

Revision is an important step in writing. First drafts are an exciting place to get ideas down. You get to try different techniques. First drafts are full of energy. When we edit, we get to direct all that energy and polish our words, so they shine just a little bit more.

I was so happy to be the editor for Rafael's poem, "Long Lost Love." He created a beautiful piece, and I greatly enjoyed reading it.

In poetry, small, even tiny, changes can make a huge impact. In our revision, Rafael and I focused on rhythm for emphasis. Rhythm in poems, metered or unmetered, is a powerful tool. Rafael's short lines have already done a great job of creating tension and heartbreak; focusing on rhythm gave us a chance to make that work go even further.

I asked Rafael to focus on three things:

One: What might the poem look like if we gave it a shape? Does it have sharp peaks or gentle hills? Are there places where it loops back on itself? We'll use this "picture" as a map to help us find places we really want to emphasize.

Two: How do we create rhythm? There are lots of different ways. The three possible ways are line breaks, punctuation, and word choice. They all work with rhythm differently, and different writers use them in varying ways and amounts. Take some time with your poem. Are there places where you feel like the rhythm is really working, where you feel like the emphasis is spot on? What about the opposite? Think of the three methods mentioned above—which ones would work at what points in your poem?

Three: The best way to become a better writer is to study other writers. Think about writers that you love. Are there any poems that inspire you? How do those writers deal with rhythm? What can we learn from them?

Rafael brought a lot of thought and care to his revision. His poem was already very powerful; adding just a few more purposeful line breaks and changing only one or two keyword choices, the poem and its powerful message came through even stronger.

I loved working with Rafael on this project; I hope you enjoy reading this poignant and beautiful poem from this young and promising poet.

Laura Schmidt

Laura Schmidt is a story-obsessed word-freak who is so excited to be part of the Young Inklings team. Stories of all shapes and types have always been the centerpiece of her life, either through books, theater or film. She personally thinks that somewhere, all stories are true, and one day she'll open a door to Narnia or fall into Wonderland. Despite this tendency, she's been granted an MFA in Writing from California Institute of the Arts and a BA in Humanities from San Jose State University. When she's not writing or inspiring young minds, Laura enjoys tackling knitting projects she will never finish.

Rafael Stankiewicz

Rafael is an eighth grader at Piedmont Middle School. He enjoys playing multiple instruments and loves to play soccer and hang outside with his friends. He's not yet sure what he wants to do when he grows up, but he knows he wants to help people. For him, writing poetry and short stories is an outlet and a place to work through any stress or problems.

Laura Schmidt: Do you normally edit, and if you do, what's your normal editing process?

> **Rafael Stankiewicz:** Usually, it's mostly just spelling and grammatical stuff. Once I get out what I'm trying to say, once I get the meaning out, I generally don't change that.

Q: Do you write mostly poetry?

> **A:** I write stories sometimes too, but mostly poetry.

Q: So how was working with an editor? How did it change things?

> **A:** It gave me a whole new perspective. My thinking for this poem was kind of one-dimensional, and I think working with an editor helped me open up my poem a little bit more.

Q: Yay! It's great to hear that. Now that you've worked with an editor, do you think you'll go back to your own work differently?

> **A:** Yeah, I do. I think I'm going to start trying to record myself speaking, to see how my poems sound, and to see if I'm really getting my message across, and to show me where I should add things.

Definitely. Another thing that can be very helpful is to have someone else read your poem out loud to you because you can hear how someone else can interpret it, and that can be a very powerful tool, too.

Q: One last question: do you have any advice or suggestions for our other young writers?

> **A:** I think just to keep an open mind throughout the process. It's not like the editor is telling you what to do, it's them helping you edit, and they really want what's best for your writing.

Long Lost Love

by

Rafael Stankiewicz

Once there was a light
Bright

Luminous

Ever present

A gift to the eyes

It was loved by the people
Far and wide

And it loved them back
But one day

The people
Stopped loving it

For no one knew

It might not always be there
Alas

The people continued
To hurt the world
Unaware of the power
They had
Unwilling to see

The monsters

They had become

The world became filthier
Pain

Distress

Erupted

The skies turned dark

The clouds turned gray
Everything

Crumbled

To the ground

Panic

Desperation
Confusion

Swept over all

Children wept

The people cried,

"What have we done?"
They promised to change
With all their hearts

But acts like this are unforgivable
Permanently etched
In the story of history
Never to be forgotten
But lost forever.

Years have passed

Now children

Ask their parents

What life used to be like
With anguish in their hearts
They begin

The long
Treacherous

Journey back

The hope

That the children will not
Suffer

The same fate

Carries them forward
Power

And knowledge

Come with great consequence
Evil left its mark
But gave joy

And opportunity

They cry

But the tears run dry

They reminisce of a better world
One that their children
Cannot fathom

A simple

Beautiful

World

An unappreciated world
That is nothing now

But a distant memory

The elders

Now spread their knowledge
Hoping to make up

For the sins

They committed
Indifference

Always catches up to you
Just as everything does
And its consequences
Cannot be evaded
The dark

Stormy sky

Stares down

Upon them
However

If one looks hard enough
There is a small sliver
Of light

To be found

The thoughts

Of what could have been
Refuse to leave.

Clarifying the Audience

Erica Morgan mentored Karishma Miranda through a revision focused on audience in Karishma's poem, "Broken Beyond Repair."

Dear Reader,

Whoever said 'a picture is worth a thousand words' clearly forgot about poetry. In a poem, a single line can bring tears to your eyes, make you break out into a wide grin, or change your whole perspective on a situation.

Imagery and metaphor are powerful tools, and Karishma used them very artfully. To better highlight her imagery, we worked on editing her poem to make the audience and tense more consistent. Originally, the speaker was very clear and developed, but it was unclear whether the narrator was addressing a general audience about her pain or speaking to the singular perpetrator of the betrayal.

Clarifying the audience helped the poem resonate with readers by showing them how they should be hearing it. Should they put themselves into the poet's shoes? Should they feel as though the poet is speaking directly to them? Should they feel like they are observing the poet's pain from a safe distance?

In this poem, the speaker's feelings are stark and intense. Her pain and frustration are palpable. It is important for the readers to know how they should feel about it. Should they feel chastised, as though responsible? Should they empathize with the narrator and feel her pain right alongside her? Should they watch the exchange and marvel at how one person can hold so much power over another?

By making a few minor pronoun and tense changes, Karishma was able to clarify the intended audience of her poem and make it much more focused and strong. Karishma ultimately changed very little of the poem as far as length, imagery, topic, tone, or structure. She mainly altered a few key pronouns and phrases, tweaked the tense, and altered her punctuation. These small changes made a huge difference in how the reader experiences the poem.

I hope that you enjoy this beautiful, sorrowful poem from a very promising young writer.

Erica Morgan

Erica Morgan is a lifelong resident of California. After graduating with a BA in Psychology, she spent time working in the field of social services before turning her full attention to writing and teaching. She is currently an instructor with the Society of Young Inklings and is also working on several collections of poetry.

Karishma Miranda

Karishma grew up in San Jose, but she does not consider herself a city girl. An only child, she grew up surrounded by her beloved pets. Her family has one dog, four chickens, and a rooster named Chump. She enjoys writing, playing the piano, and drawing.

Erica Morgan: Do you have a favorite poem?

Karishma Miranda: No, I actually don't read very much poetry. I read mainly fictional books like *The Fault in Our Stars* and *The Hunger Games.*

Q: Do you tend to edit your own work?

A: I write and then I edit a while later. I don't enjoy it very much because it can be boring, but I do it because it makes the story better.

Q: Do you prefer writing poetry to writing short stories?

A: No, not really. I enjoy writing stories more because I feel like it's easier to be more thorough in a story than it is in a poem.

Q: Do you have a writing goal like being published or writing a book?

A: I would love to finish the book I started in fourth grade. It's about a dog who is a spy.

Q: What is your favorite topic to write about?

> **A:** I like to write about happiness because it makes me feel good to write about something happy sometimes. Sometimes sad poems just happen, though. I wrote "Broken Beyond Repair" without really setting out to. My poems do tend to be sadder than my stories, now that I think about it.

Q: What made you want to submit "Broken Beyond Repair"?

> **A:** I think it's the best poem I've written. I wrote it specifically for the Inklings Book Contest, and I think it came out well. I wrote a lot of poetry when I was younger, and this one is more recent and has better vocabulary.

Broken Beyond Repair

by

Karishma Miranda

As I sit on the rough sand
Gazing at the shallow waves
As still as a dead bee
I cannot move, only wait
Wait for the one who will never arrive

She said she wouldn't go
But as the sun rises
I sink lower
Longing for her appearance
But she's nowhere to be seen

In the mild glow
Of the morning sun
I'm sitting here
All alone
Abandoned and deserted
Detached from everything;
Everything I once had

I am waiting for her
The one who won't arrive
She tore me down
Into thousands of tiny pieces
Unable to be repaired
No one can mend me

I'm destroyed.
I'm broken beyond repair.

Metaphor

Meridith Donahue mentored Sophia Zalewski through a revision focused on metaphor in Sophia's poem, "The Storm Inside Her."

Dear Reader,

I had a great time revising Sophia's poem with her. "The Storm Inside Her" is full of images that carry great emotional weight; Sophia compares her character's pain to the intensity of a storm. Sophia's words draw the reader in with her strong use of metaphor. A metaphor is a figure of speech that makes a comparison between two things that aren't related, but share similarities.

Storms and emotional pain may not seem similar at first, but take a word like "sting," which Sophia uses to describe the "bite of clashing waves" and "the slap of the hand." The right word can easily showcase the similarities between two contrasting things.

Sophia and I focused on strengthening the storm metaphor in her poem. Here are three areas to pay attention to if you want to strengthen the use of metaphor in your own writing: word choice, making comparisons, and line length.

First and most important: word choice. Think about the metaphor you're using and words that are associated with that topic. Sophia brainstormed storm words and phrases, and she replaced words that didn't relate to the metaphor with stronger words, such as "whip," "violent splashes," and "pattering." These three examples contribute to Sophia's storm metaphor in different ways.

This leads to the second tip: examining your subjects and making comparisons. Sophia and I examined her poem's arc and lined it up with the girl's greatest moment of pain. Next, we talked about how storms start with a drizzle of rain, and then get stronger, with booming thunder and lightning. After a while, the rain trickles off into nothing once more. Sophia's challenge was to make sure that the girl's emotional intensity matched the storm's intensity.

Whether you write stories or poems, it's good to look at the length of your lines and stanzas (or sentences and paragraphs). Read your poem (or story) out loud. Does your line sound like you thought it would? Are there any words you stumble over? Sophia shortened some of her lines to increase their power, like quick, pelting drops of rain. Some of her lines are longer, like a steady, drizzling rain. Paying attention to line length helped Sophia achieve the right effect to strengthen her metaphor.

Sophia's storm metaphor leaps off the page, and I hope you'll enjoy reading "The Storm Inside Her" as much as I did! With a little work, I know you can create great metaphors of your own, too.

Meridith Donahue

Meridith Donahue's love of books and writing began at an early age when she would take as many books out of the library as she could carry. In junior high, she began taking voice lessons and auditioned for her very first musical. Ever since then, she's been on stage performing in or choreographing plays and musicals. She co-led her college's comedy improv team and got a poem published in her school's literary magazine. She's never given up on either passion and got a BA in English Studies from Northern Illinois, as well as an MFA in Writing for Children and Young Adults from Hamline University. When she's not teaching, writing, or performing, you can find her reading or watching BBC shows.

Sophia Zalewski

Sophia is a Piedmont Middle School eighth grader who is energetic and loves animals. She enjoys literature and writing, and she composed a poem illustrating the similarities of a storm and a girl who is mourning the loss of a loved one. Sophia plays violin and runs track and cross country for her school, yet continues to find time to write. She is extremely excited for the Inklings Book to be published, and can't wait to read all of the poems and stories.

Meridith Donahue: What was your inspiration for this poem?

Sophia Zalewski: I wanted to write about something that would be powerful, so I started writing about a storm and connected it to how someone felt to make it deeper.

Q: What changed when you revised to strengthen the metaphors in your poem?

A: Definitely the word choice, and that changed the feeling of the poem.

Q: How did you discover the girl's pain was really a loss?

A: When I was reading through the poem, I tried to make myself feel like the reader instead of the author. The first time I read through it, it sounded like a different pain. It could have been someone who died.

Q: When did you start writing?

A: A long time ago, but it was me telling stories to my mom and her writing them down. I liked stories a lot when I was younger. I wrote one about a girl. It was her birthday, and she went to an amusement park. She and her friends realized that they had gone on all the rides. The owner told them that it would cost them $10,000, but it was really a trick to set them up for a birthday party.

Q: What is your favorite book or series?

A: It's a tie between *Harry Potter* and the *Divergent* series.

Q: What Hogwarts house would you be in?

A: I want to say Gryffindor, but I don't think I would. I think I'd probably be in Ravenclaw.

Q: If you could have any superpower, what would it be?

A: Super speed or the ability to freeze time. Super speed because it would be really cool to run around the world, and if you're really hungry for really good pasta, you could just run to Italy and run back really quickly.

Ability to freeze time because if you're in a situation where you have to think of a response, you can pause and think about what you're going to do. If you're in the middle of a test, you can pause and think about your answer if the bell is going to ring. You could also get work done really quickly. The second before you have to do something, you can pause and relax for a while.

Q: What types of stories do you normally like to write?

A: All types of stories. Sometimes, I like mysteries and adventures. I also like writing about the scary stuff, too, because that's interesting to me.

Q: Why do you enjoy writing?

A: I like stories. I like reading them and writing them. It's fun to be able to get involved. If you're writing about something that didn't actually happen, you can write about it and go to another world. That's kind of cool.

The Storm Inside Her

by

Sophia Zalewski

The wind whips her face,
A reminder of the pain she felt.
A sting that resonates like that of a slap of the hand
Or the bite of clashing waves.
Violent splashes of water that arise from her shore,
They are tipped with white.
Murderously crashing to the cadence of her heart
Which fills with sorrow and loss.
Wherever one looks, they see this surrounding mourn,
Draped across the sky like curtains
Waiting to be drawn.
No birds fly here,
Caressing the sky with their wings.

The pattering rain dampens their feathers too much to fly.

On the outside, it is a sunny day.

On the inside, a storm.

Playing with Rhythm

Loraine McCormick mentored Colin Chu through a revision focused on rhythm in Colin's poem, "Ten."

Dear Reader,

Colin's poem immediately caught my eye—even before I read it! He created a visual poem in the shape of the number ten. I was intrigued by the image, which corresponds nicely with the title of his poem, "Ten."

It's a wonderful, whimsical poem that highlights the differences between a boy and his grandfather, each one contributing in his own way to the fabric of life. It celebrates the important contributions we all make, whether young or old.

In our revision, Colin and I focused on rhythm, rearranging words to build a more lyrical beat and to give the lines more symmetry. When you create a visual poem, you don't need to create rhyming words or even a rhythm. I saw an opportunity, though, for Colin to retain the uniqueness of the numerical shape and to also introduce a more rhythmic quality, without eliminating too many original words.

While Colin and I worked on his poem, I talked to him about the analogy of rearranging furniture within his room. You might have the basics (the bed, bookshelf, rug, lamp, etc.), but perhaps the bed is too close to the window, and the shelf is too close to the door. By taking those same pieces and simply rearranging them a bit, you can create a more successful, harmonious arrangement. And that's what we did with Colin's poem! We created more rhythm, more of a beat, by rearranging the words to achieve more symmetry. We also read the words aloud, counting the number of syllables to see which arrangement sounded best.

And by eliminating just a few words (mainly conjunctions like "and" and "but") and adding in just a couple new words, we rearranged the "room" of his poem. We made sure that the first line of almost every stanza started with the words "For Every...." Take a look at the last line of every stanza. You'll see that Colin worked to place just three words on most of those lines: "I jump 10!" or "He reads 10!"

The shape of the number ten is still there, and now it's still fun to look at, but also fun to read aloud! I know you'll enjoy reading Colin's poem.

Loraine McCormick

Loraine McCormick teaches creative writing through the Society of Young Inklings, and she edits children's books. She is a member of the Society of Children's Book Writers and Illustrators. She has a BA in Advertising, with a concentration in English, from San Jose State University. She has worked in publishing as a copywriter and in high tech as a technical editor. Currently, she is writing several children's picture books, as well as a middle-grade novel. She's raised two sons and lives in San Jose, California, with her husband and a golden doodle named Ginger.

Colin Chu

Colin lives in Palo Alto, California. He is eight years old and likes to swim. He also likes to play trumpet and run. When he grows up, he might like to be a writer.

Loraine McCormick: Where did you get the idea for this poem? I love that it is a visual poem.

> **Colin Chu:** We were reading a book in school called *Hate that Cat* by Sharon Creech. Our homework was to write a poem based on our favorite type of poetry, and I decided to write a visual poem in the shape of the number 10.

Q: Your poem is a lovely tribute to your grandfather. Tell me about that.

> **A:** I was trying to think of something to write about, and then I just came up with the idea of writing about my grandfather. He teaches me a lot, and it is very helpful.

Q: Do you think that you'll write more visual poems in the future?

> **A:** Yes, I would like to write some more visual poems. I'll just see what happens.

Q: How did you feel about the revision process?

> **A:** I felt better because you could help me get better at writing.

Q: Did you change more or less than you expected to change?

A: I changed just the right amount. I changed what I was expecting to change.

Q: What do you like best about writing poetry?

A: I like how you don't need to rhyme all the words in a poem. You showed me when you are making a visual poem that sometimes we can also create a rhythm by rearranging where some of the words are on a line.

Ten

by
Colin Chu

For every step
he takes,
leaning
on the rail,
I jump 10!

For every sign
he sees,
squinting
through eye glasses,
I see 10!

For every word
he hears
adjusting
his hearing aids,
I hear 10!

For every
math problem I solve,
struggling with variables,
he solves 10!

For every
Chinese character I write,
barely recalling the strokes,
he writes 10!

For every
book I read,
distracted by all the new words,
he reads 10!

His body is getting s l o w e r,
but his brain is still so much faster.
My grandfather is, after all,
my age times 10!